BREAKING MICHEAL

A Hard Lesson For My Sister's Husband

Author Dixit

AD

The characters and events portrayed in this book are fictitious. Any similarity to real persons, living or dead, is coincidental and not intended by the author.

CONTENTS

BREAKING MICHEAL

A Hard Lesson For My Sister's Husband

CHAPTER 1 – BALLS IN DISTRESS

Not many people looked in the direction, perhaps because of the loud metal music filling the lounge and the sexy sight of half-clad models twisting around shiny silver poles, but me, me, I see everything.

I narrowed my view to catch more details and judge if this is just the usual guys-hitting-on-girls thing or another episode of some random Mr Jerk.

For whatever reasons, there has been an inflow of idiots into Club G4 lately, like it happens when a joint starts rising up the charts and getting attention.

The one thing that has made G4 my favourite hangout spot is for how coded it is. Loud music, but calm. Big club, but not overcrowded. But since the fame is rising, jerks are coming along with the sexy people of Northampton that make the place colourful.

My elbows rested on the blue table, chin resting on the back of my left palm and my right hand held the cup a few centimetres away from my lips as I visually investigated what's going on between the lady in blue denim bum short and the muscular fool covered in tattoos holding her hands seemingly against her wish.

Yes, I'm sure, she's bothering her! The girl is trying to wrestle her right hand out of his grasp, and she isn't strong enough. But I am!

All this while Clara's eyes were locked on the male stud doing a striptease on a table for four middle-aged women. I stood up and walked away before she noticed something else had my attention.

The mistake the barbie girl on blue shorts is making is trying to talk sense into a numb skull. That approach never works with these idiots. You don't talk them to reason, you subdue them to it!

In a very swift move, which I have practised and used many times, I pulled down the zip of his shorts and reached for his balls. The fool wore boxers, so I pulled the band out and lower with my left hand and reached for his genitals with my right hand. In approximately five seconds, his balls were in my hands — in a tight fist!

We started gaining attention.

It happened too fast for him, as I pulled his balls with high traction, he dropped the girl's hands, but couldn't get hold of mine, being in sudden anguish.

Instantly and involuntarily, he bent forward to cushion the pain, but it was no use — as I pulled harder, intent on ripping off his genitals from his groin.

Squeals? A lot of it!

He squealed and yelled and winced and cried out loud enough to pierce through the music blasting from the giant speakers hanging from the ceiling of the club lounge.

First, I had saved the girl, and she was glad, and smiling, and thankful for my interference. The eyes on us now could figure that I was her knight in shining armour.

"Pleaseeeeeeeeeeeeee..." He begged me, nervously holding the helm of his shorts, scared, confused and languishing in pain.

"Shut up you fool!" I screamed back at him, angrily. "We don't want jerks here!"

Clara stood up now and approached. It's her friend — me, at the centre of this exciting scene and she wondered how the hell things went from us both enjoying ourselves at a table to me grabbing some random guy's balls.

"Martha!" Clara screamed my name at me and started laughing. She can be quite a knucklehead sometimes, gets entertained with almost everything. Up until she showed up, my face has been knotted in a frown, full of anger, but Clara's laughter can be very contagious. I let out a forced smile, or rather, a provoked one, but I was angry still.

"I don't know where these bitches are coming from, but they better behave or I will be ripping their balls apart, one by one."

That wasn't enough information to let Clara know what led to this, but she now knows I was provoked to it. She and now a few bystanders smirked and expected to hear more. One thing was clear — they were loving my superwoman show, even the men among them.

"He wouldn't let me be," The girl explained to Clara and the others, since all I focused on was yanking this idiot's balls off. I clamped my thumb around the base of his dick, as tears now welled up on his eyes.

"The idiot's cock is even small!" I blurted out. Everyone around laughed. "See!" I said as I pulled cock out through the zip. My rapidly growing audience laughed wildly, while I tightened my fist on his balls.

He shed the first tear.

"Awww," Clara puffed, pressing her palms on her large juicy boobs. "He is crying!"

"He deserves to," I angrily replied.

Amazingly, no one came to his aid, despite his tears. Not that anyone could get him out of that fierce grip though. He would only get out when I let him, when I want.

All the masculinity and manliness with which he previously bothered the lady disappeared. It's incredible how fast men can transform from a testosterone-overbearing bastard into a scared little kitten — when you grab them by the balls.

This is my signature move, and it has never failed me.

"Beg her, you fool, tell her you are sorry!"

The idiot could not even turn properly to face the lady. He was so much in pains he couldn't stand straight again, nor move his upper body. He only managed to turn his head sideways towards the girl.

"Please forgive me, I'm sorry," he managed to say through tears and squeals.

"Awww..." the lady blushed.

Now everyone knew he wronged her, and they knew what sort of offence he must have committed, like any other young testosterone-driven idiot of his age can be guilty of with such a hot sexy body flaunted in a skimpy dress.

"I am not impressed!" I tightened my fist again and he yelped. His cock and balls were in the open for all to see.

The veins on his scrotum appeared to be in distress as they darted in all directions on the surface of his shiny balls. He is an idiot, but at least well shaven. There was rarely any strand of hair around his genitals, which made viewing them more pleasurable.

The key to his submission was the grip on those balls, and I wouldn't let go.

The thin wall of his scrotal sac turned pink, and from pink, it turned red. Red and shiny. Very shiny.

"Apologize like you mean it. Let it come from deep down within you, not just because I'm asking you too."

He barely heard what I said, I think. His head continued hanging lower and lower as he sobbed. Tears ran down his face, but I remained fierce and resolute on teaching him a lesson he will never forget in his life.

I can't comprehend why men see women as being weak when it's them who have their eggs outside — a vulnerable design via which mother nature intends for us to keep them humble, I believe.

He couldn't turn his face towards her now, but could still manage to speak.

"Please... Err...." He mumbled.

"Look at you. You don't even know her name, yet you were dragging her like you are her father or something, you worm. Ask for her name and apologize properly!"

"Errr..." He cried and shed some more tears, "Please Ma'am, what is your name?"

Ha. People can be respectful, when you make them.

The tone of his voice and his body language was now that of submission, eager to do whatever I command.

"Catriona. My name is Catriona," the lady replied, feeling empowered now and happy to see the idiot suffering for his insolence.

It's his balls I was squeezing in my hands, not his lungs, but for some reason, he struggled with breathing — which is none of my business. I will teach him this lesson. He has to learn.

After taking a few moments to breathe, he attempted again.

"Please, Catriona, please forgive me," he panted, "I will never do that again!"

"You will never do what? Tiny dick!"

Folks laughed at the word 'Tiny dick' and stared at his dick in my hands. It was extra-tiny now, given the pain I was subjecting it to.

"I will never disturb you again. Please forgive me."

"So, you will go on to disturb someone else?" I asked, tightening my grip on his balls again, to which he yelped.

"No, please, I won't."

"You can call me 'Goddess.'"

"No, Goddess, I won't bother any woman again!"

"Why? Tell me one good reason why you won't do this again."

He took a moment to breathe.

"Err... B... Because It's not right."

"Yeah, it's not, but give me more."

"Err," he panted, "Because I don't want this to happen to me again."

"Of course, you don't. Give me more."

I was thrilling the crowd and I was loving it.

"Look at the size of your cock, and tell me why you won't bother any woman again."

"I won't disturb any woman again because I have a tiny cock."

"Aha!" I gasped.

Some people behind smuggled their body through the mini-crowd forward to catch a better view. They did pity him because he was obviously in pains, but I was providing entertainment with it, so, they were caught in between feeling pity for him and being entertained.

"Say it louder. They didn't hear you."

Sure, they did, but I just wanted to humiliate him further.

"I WON'T DISTURB ANY WOMAN EVER AGAIN BECAUSE I HAVE A TINY COCK!" he said, actually screaming so loud, frustrated and obeying me so I could get what I want and release him from the sadistic hold.

Honestly, I should have been impressed with that like everyone else was, but I know the real reason he did as I commanded is because of the pain and discomfort.

"Just imagine," I said to my spectators, "If with such a tiny dick, he is harassing women at every turn, what would have happened if he had a big dick, something fitting for a man of his age?"

"That's why he is tiny!" some guy said from the back.

Following my cue, they began to mock and make jokes of him, even the men among them.

And now, they all began to see me for the hot and fiery woman that I am. I bet sitting in Club G4 would not be the same again for me. Not with this face of a strict disciplinarian registering on their minds.

I was enjoying my brute show of power but knew it had to end soon, for I wouldn't want this fucker to faint on my grip.

His head was lower than my butt now as he hanged it low in distress, only sobbing now, not being able to make intelligible statements again. I was squeezing the life out of him and I knew it. I just wanted to be sure that when I let go, the lesson I taught him would be embossed on his soul for the rest of his life. That's how I like to treat these worms, with a lesson they will never forget!

Besides, not only Clara now, but everyone watching was begging me to please let go, including the lady who was being harassed by this idiot. Satisfactorily, I had done a good job putting him in his place.

Should I just let go like that? I asked myself. No. This needs a grand ending. Ah. Yes. I will take his knicker and boxer shorts as spoils of war!

I stared briefly at Clara and then the faces of the people begging me, snarled at the thought of the sinister way I intend to end this.

"Okay, okay, people. I believe he has learnt his lessons!" I puffed.

"I hope he has the courage to come to G4 again..." some lady muttered.

I cleared my throat.

"Hey, hey! Look at me looser!" He couldn't. He wanted to, but honestly couldn't. He was just too weak now. "So, here's the thing. I will let you go, in exchange for your knicker and boxers. Deal?"

"Martha!" Clara sighed heavily through the cacophony of laughter and idle comments.

"Don't 'Martha' me," I jokingly replied. "I'm offering him a way out. He can take it or we can do this till he drops unconscious."

He sighed heavily, muttered his agreement, but it wasn't loud enough, and I wouldn't take that. But luckily for him, I was holding his balls as tight as I ever could, any more pressure might just burst his scrotum and send his balls bouncing on the floor, so, I just had to maintain the grip like that and hope he would find the strength to talk before he faints.

"Yes, Goddess! Please take them!" he said loud enough, straining himself so much for strength to speak, and pronouncing the words slowly, one by one, like a toddler learning to speak.

He unbuckled his belt and let his knicker fall to his ankles, then slowly he stepped his legs out of it.

I bent down and picked his knicker, throwing it over my left shoulder, like a proud warrior.

He couldn't stand anymore and collapsed to the floor, therefore, I had to hunker down, not letting go of my grip on his scrotum.

"Your boxers. That's mine too. Give it to me."

Of course, he was going to do that, but he needed to rest a little before he would find the strength to pull it off. I wanted him to do that by himself, not I or anyone else doing that for him.

Now that he knows the terms for his release, it's on him to do the needful.

His breathing became heavy and noisy, and pretty much everyone was bothered for him, but I remained stern, so, no one could interrupt.

He hooked his thumbs into the sides of his boxer shorts and pulled it off his waist, and in one last move that demanded all the strength he had left, he folded his knees up to his chest and pulled the boxers off and handed it over to me.

I proudly collected it from him on the roar of the spectators on seeing his nakedness. He was buried in great humiliation, but couldn't be bothered by being so embarrassed anymore, he just wanted relief.

"Please, Goddess, forgive me, please," he managed to say again, and I finally let go of his balls.

He rolled on his back and his chest expanded and fell as he

drew in his first full breath since I had his balls in my hands. He couldn't even be bothered for his nudity. The one thing on his mind was to breathe. Just breathe.

With his knicker and boxers, I walked majestically away from the scene back to my seat, cheered on every step I took. This is one awesome moment I will never forget.

Clara watched in awe as I walked back to the seat, but she wasn't done staring at the dude I just stripped naked. Others weren't too.

Back on my seat, I took a shot of tequila and laid the prize beside me.

After Clara had her fill with feasting her eyes on the naked humiliated dude, she came back to sit with me.

"Girl! You're one hell of a crazy bitch! I can't believe what just happened!"

I could only laugh. I can believe it. I know how to fuck men up.

"You are returning those to him, right?" she said, pointing at the knicker and boxers which I had now folded.

"No! These are mine!"

"Are you kidding me?" Clara asked, laughing wildly.

"No, I'm not!"

"Damn!"

"Yeah, damn!"

Just then, my phone rang. My sister — Annabel.

Her voice was devoid of the usual lustre as she asked if I'm at home because she's on her way already.

"Anna! What's going on?" I asked.

"It's Micheal!"

Oh, not again! Annabel and I were raised together. I know her. She as soft and loving hearted as anyone could be. I on the other could be a bitch sometimes, but things have never gotten out of hands between us because, when I'm boiling, she'd be calm. When I'm sulking and harbouring unhealthy feelings, she'd put our differences aside and go out of her way to make up with me. And that's how she is with everyone! My sister is a sweet person. I hate to see a man make life difficult for her. Oh men, pfffft! I dislike them!

"I'm at the club, but I'm leaving right away. We'll meet at home," I said and ended the call.

"Clara, gotta leave."

"Why?"

"My sister!"

"Okay," Clara replied. "I've had more than enough fun here today, thanks to you, 'Goddess!'" she said, laughing as she mentioned the word.

I picked up my wallet and the knicker and boxers prize of domination.

As Clara and I walked out of Club G4, all eyes were on me and folks cheered me.

That looser? He was still on the floor, but back in his senses — only that he was filled with shame.

He covered his face with both hands and wondered how to get himself out of that low place. I paused my steps and gloated over him. He stared briefly at me and lowered his gaze.

I felt pity for him, but not enough to return his clothes. Those belong to me now.

By the way, he deserves it. Just considering whatever it is going that got Anna on the way to my house made me even angrier at men. I stared at the fool on the floor and felt like removing his shirt too, but I had already done enough.

The issues between Annabel and her husband is now a concern for me, and I found myself thinking, as I looked at the guy I just dealt with, that maybe this is what Micheal Brown needs?

Yeah. Maybe this is what he needs.

I would have stepped in myself a long time ago, but Anna keeps making excuses for him and never wants things to escalate. The last time I was mad and wanted to insult him on the phone, Anna quickly yanked the phone out of my hand and cut the call.

Well, one thing is certain, no one can mess up with my sister.

Not when she has me.

As I took one last condescending look at the dude I stripped naked, I imagined Micheal in his stead. That image stuck in my head as Clara and I walked out of Club G4.

No one will frustrate my sister. Not when she has me.

CHAPTER 2 – ANNABEL?

Clara and I proudly stepped into my blood-red Ford Mustang and I drove away from G4. Clara's excitement prevented my mind from getting clouded with Anna's situation brewing in my mind. She just couldn't stop talking about it.

"This is one crazy stunt," she said to me as she stared at the knicker and boxers. "I wish I am as bold as you are, Martha."

My head swelled with pride. That was confidence-boosting. The spectators were amazed. Clara is still amazed. I am a great woman.

I made a turn into Clara's street and dropped her in front of her house. It would take about twenty minutes to get to my house now and my thoughts were back on Annabel.

Holding the steering with my left hand, I slowed down and picked the phone from my wallet with my right hand. It was Annabel calling.

"That's okay, I'm just a couple of blocks away now," I said to her after she informed me she just arrived. Good thing she doesn't have to wait for long.

Dress? Anna doesn't go out in dresses! My heart bumped as I glanced at her while still behind the steering and pulling over. I ran out immediately I did, without even picking my purse.

"Anna!" I gasped as I took her in my alms. "What is it, Anna!"

"Micheal!" she puffed. "Micheal."

"Again?"

"Yes, again."

Her face was flushed and her cheeks pink. One could almost see the blood beneath her skin.

"Did he touch you?"

"No, but almost."

"What's this then?" I asked, touching her neck and Inspecting the light pink stripe.

"Ricochet."

I raised my eyebrows, demanding for the details.

"He lost his damn mind again and smashed his phone against the wall. The back cover came for my neck."

"Oh fuck!" I heaved a sigh. "Same dope?"

She nodded.

Before they got married, Annabel and I had no idea Micheal is a drug addict. He had his act together so well all we saw was a fine gentleman with six packs to show for his hard work in the gym.

Just barely a year into the marriage, a six-heads hydra of six different kinds of addictive substances reared its head and was beginning to threaten my sister's safety. I don't know how this thing works on other people, but I know how it works on Micheal. It transforms him into a randomly violent beast. Throwing things and screaming, unprovoked, and eager to throw a punch to whoever attempts to curtail his rage.

My mind was distraught. I turned the doorknob down before remembering I hadn't opened the door, and the key is in my purse, and the purse is in my car. I puffed.

"Let me get the key, please," I said to her, not being able to hide the sadness filling up my heart like floodwaters claiming the streets.

I dashed to the car, opened the door and grabbed my purse, but then I laid my eyes on something else — the knicker and boxers I seized from the fool in G4.

For a moment, I froze, bodily, but got super active in the realm of imagination. I saw myself again in G4 and the slides moved slowly. How I noticed that foolish boy whose name I don't even know. How I subdued him. How I publicly humiliated him. I even made him call me Goddess and bow to me. And the lady whom I rescued, how did she react? Grateful! Yeah. She was grateful I interfered. And the spectators? Entertained. They pitied him but enjoyed every minute I spent dominating him.

I successfully saved a random girl from a random pest, and here is my own sister living in fear because her husband has become a threat? And all I will do is comfort her? No way. Not when I can rescue her.

The thoughts began to solidify. I picked up the knicker and boxers and now, they held more meaning than just being pieces of clothing. They are proofs of my strength and what I can achieve with it. They are proof that I can subdue men. They are proof that I can rescue my sister from the monster her husband is turning into.

When I walked away from Anna towards the car, it was with a depressed soul, but as I walked back, I did with strength and vigour, pride and confidence.

Annabel looked bemused, wondering what changed so quickly and why was I suddenly smiling.

I glided past her to the door and opened it. "Come in, sis," I said to her, happily.

She stared at me from head to toe, amused, bemused.

"Martha?"

I dropped the clothes on the sofa and dashed to the fridge to fetch something chill for us to drink. Irish whiskey.

"Martha?" she called again while I set the cups on a coffee table.

"Martha!"

"Yes, Anna!"

I looked and saw her holding and spreading out the knicker and boxers.

"What is this?" She asked, "Whose are this?"

"Some fool who experienced what your silly husband is about to experience!"

Her gaze lingered on my face.

"It belongs to someone I stripped naked," I said, so casually.

"You stripped someone naked?"

"Yes, I did. A man."

"You stripped a man naked?"

"Yes, I did. A fool."

She shook her head and refused to sit, though I did already and even took a sip of whiskey. She just couldn't wrap her head around what I'm saying.

"Are you high, Martha?" she asked me with a grin.

"No, I'm not. But Micheal is, and is about to be put in his place!"

I stretched my feet and curled my toes. "You are a sweet person. You don't deserve such an idiot!"

Annabel laughed.

"Wait sis, Micheal later. This first. Who owns these clothes, why did you strip him naked, how did you even do that, what the hell just happened?"

"Anna! Slow down!" I blurted, laughing out loud. "Which one of your forty questions do I answer first?"

"Serially. Start from the first and move down along."

This is what sisters are for. We hadn't even spent up to twenty minutes together, and she was now smiling already. The fear and sadness beaming on her face when I first saw her had fizzled away without us both noticing at exactly which moment it did.

"Will you sit first?"

"Nah," she shrugged her shoulders, picked her cup of whiskey, sipped and dropped it back down on the table. "Start talking now, girl," she snarled at me like mother would when we were little girls.

"Okay, okay," I started. "You know my friend; Clara.."

"Yeah,"

"Okay. She and I were at G4. We were having fun and nodding our heads to the music when I noticed this idiot holding some girl's wrist and refusing to let go despite her futile attempts to wrestle her hands away from his grip. You know, she was sort of barbie doll and he was infatuated and in his mind must have been decided to have her at all cost."

"Sexually harassing her?"

"Exactly!"

Now that she was beginning to have an idea what happened, she took a seat beside me and sipped some more whiskey.

However ridiculous what I did might have initially looked to her, now she knew I did it to save someone. I am a hero.

I quickly dashed to the kitchen again to fetch some cookies and some juice. Annabel and I are lounging now, and it's fun.

"Wait, wait," She giggled. "You mean, you grabbed his balls, just like that?"

I laughed back at her. "Yes, just like that."

She shook her head in awe.

"See," I continued, "That move renders them powerless. Chill for a second and imagine how it would feel like if you had your fallopian tubes and ovaries outside?"

Annabel lost form laughing her ass out, almost tumbling off the couch.

"Aha! Now you have an idea of what I'm talking about."

"That would be so bad. Nothing else can render one more vulnerable than that!"

"Exactly. That's how vulnerable it makes men, having their eggs outside!" I said to her.

The frown on her face was completely replaced with smiles and laughter, and she was now looking like the Annabel that I have known all my life; sweet, happy, lively, Annabel — except for having stepped out of the house in a dress which is not characteristic of her. But that was okay, before that crazy husband of hers gives her a terrible scar or does something far worse.

"But that would have been enough. The pain taught him a lesson for sure. But now stripping him naked? Whew. And the folks in there watched you do that to him without coming to his aid?

"No one dared to challenge the Lioness!"

Hahahaa... "Lioness!" Annabel gasped.

I stretched my hands towards her.

"Anna, give me your keys."

She paused and looked confused, wondering what I was up to.

"W- What i..."

"Anna!" I interrupted and didn't let her say what she wanted to. "Your keys first."

"House key?"

"Yes, house key. Give it to me!"

Still looking lost, she dropped the key on my palm.

"Thank you," I said to her and threw a cookie in my mouth.

"Sweetheart, what's going on?" she asked.

"You just wait and see, you will thank me later."

Given the story I just narrated to her, and my present action, she connected the dots and knew what I had in mind.

"Martha!"

"Don't 'Martha' me, just relax and watch. The lord works in mysterious ways!"

A wide grin broke through the brief bland expression on her face.

"This has nothing to do with the lord. This is you just being... Just being... Errrrrrrr"

I narrowed my view and stared at her from underneath my eyes lids.

"Errrrr... Words fail me!"

"Goddess? Is that the word?" I suggested.

"Martha, you are crazy. You crushed a stranger's balls and made him call you Goddess. Wheeew!"

"Micheal is about to do the same!" I blurted and poured myself a cup of pineapple juice.

Annabel looked lost, with a mixture of fear and hope on her face. She paused and looked straight into my eyes, but wouldn't say a word."

"Anna, Anna!" I tugged her.

She was lost in thoughts.

"You are joking, right?"

"No, I'm not!" I replied and waved the seized clothes in her face, "Does this look like a joke?"

She heaved a heavy sigh and shook her head sideways, "No, it doesn't."

"Just calm down, relax here and wait. That's all you have to do. When I have Micheal grovelling at my feet, naked, humiliated and conquered, I will call you and ask you to come over."

"What if something goes wrong? What if he overpowers you? Martha, I can't risk you going near him right now. I ran out of the house. I literally did."

"I know. You don't wear dresses out, Anna."

Beneath her fears and worries, I saw that hope flickering, wishing this script would just play out as it just did for me at G4.

"It's getting me mad, Anna, that this maniac has you cowering just at the thought of him. I will put an end to this, whether you like it or not." I got really mad and my confidence ran up the scale. "I don't care who the fuck he is, he will come down at my feet, I promise you that."

My words inspired some faith in Annabel and colour seemed to return to her face.

"Please, my dear, just be careful!"

"I swear to you, Anna, when you come over to see this dude, you will pity him. You will not believe what I would have turned him into."

"Jeez! Martha, you are just as fierce as mum. Even more!"

I winked and held the cookie plate towards her. She picked one and threw it in her mouth.

"Relax. Just relax and let the lord work in mysterious ways!"

"You are crazy, Martha!"

We laughed and for the first time since she got to my house, I saw her being joyous.

"It's a good thing today is Friday. He isn't going to work tomorrow and Sunday."

"So?"

"That's enough to lay the foundation."

Annabel let a sigh again and picked a cookie.

I went into the kitchen and the store to check If I was low on supplies. I wasn't. The last shopping I did was just about 8 days ago and I bought stuff enough to last for a whole month and even more.

I paused at the back entrance into the living room and stared at Annabel. She threw her right foot forward and bounced on the couch as she playfully picked cookies and drank juice. My sister is happy again!

"I have everything you will need. Food, drinks and all."

She nodded and picked another cookie. I loved the state she was in now. What I earlier saw broke my heart. But now, she's getting her groove on.

As I walked into the bedroom to check on my supply of pads, Annabel rose from the couch fetched herself another box of juice. Her worries were gone.

This is how happy she deserves to be, and I will now make sure of that. We have always stood up for each other, and that's not about to stop.

I showed her the key to the door and dropped it on the small dining table. Then I walked her around to show her a few things. It's not her first time in my house, of course, she has come many times, and even more recently since Micheal's violence began. But it will probably be her first time staying days alone at my house, without my presence there with her. But that's for her good, though.

She took the dress off and went into the bathroom. My blue pinafore dress fit snuggly on her body since we are of the same size.

I filled my handbag with a few things I would need and got ready to leave. I confidently stared into Annabel's eyes and inspired more hope.

"Anytime fear tries to creep into your heart, look at these and remember what I am capable of!" I said to her, pointing at the clothes of the dude I stripped naked.

She lingered her stare on it and then turned back at me with a beautiful smile on her face.

"Still, I'd be calling to check on you though."

"No problem."

We held each other in a long embrace. The purity of her heart warmed me up. There's just this aura about her. An aura of peace and calmness. I remember some night when we were little. Anna and I ran into the woods and got lost. It was a weekend we were spending at Granny's and we always loved it there because there was a lot of space to play in.

As the sun went down and darkness set in, we were both afraid but Anna hugged me so tightly and my fears disappeared. When mum and dad found us, we were writing alphabets on the sand.

Anna has that sweet energy.

She locked the door behind me and I got into my Ford Mustang. I know a dungeon on Bridle Road, and it's just twenty minutes drive from here.

"Hey, Martha!" Wilfred says to me.

Wilfred and his wife, Freya, own and run the dungeon. They are both dominants and I always wonder how that works for them. What's more important is the beautiful space they provide for play and the regular kinky events they run. It helps the local community to strengthen. Attending such local munches has been very instrumental in bringing out the Domme in me. The dungeon, munchies, play parties... These are parts of me that Clara and Annabel don't know, but that I guess they soon will.

"Hello, Wilfred."

He kisses the back of my hand as I lift it for him.

One of the keepers is polishing leather gears outside as Wilfred walks me in.

"And Freya?"

"She's out on a meeting with Dr Alfred."

Ah, the almighty Alfred. Voice deep like that of a bass guitar. Reverberates when he talks.

"We are having another live rope session next Friday," he says to me excitedly, knowing how much I love Shibari.

"Oh, great!" I puffed. Hopefully, I'd be back by then.

"Going somewhere?"

"Yes, and that's what brought me here. I need weapons of bondage!"

Wilfred spares a grin from the corner of his mouth and with his husky voice asks me, "Someone is in trouble?"

I smirked, "Oh yes, and he doesn't even know it yet."

The sales store is a large room with a vast array of BDSM toys and equipment. Almost anything and everything can be found there. Though there are always free toys in the play areas, folks always come in here to buy their own toys.

I pointed at buttplugs, ropes, smoother harness, bullwhip, cane.

"I want this, this, this, this and that too," I said to Wilfred, pointing at the blindfold hood, mouth gag, handcuffs and heavy D-ring chain and a big padlock.

"Martha!" Wilfred gasps.

"Don't 'Martha' me, just bring them."

"Yes, your highness," he says to me, slightly bowing forward, playfully.

Then I point at the extra-large metal bondage cage, made out of pure steel.

Wilfred heaved a sigh. "Damn!"

I smiled and brought out my card. He saw the excitement and eagerness in me. Everywhere I turn, it's Micheal I'm seeing. In chains, wearing a hood. In a cage, naked and oh? Fuck! How did I forget?

"Wilfred, a tiny penis cage. I want a tiny penis cage too. Tiny."

"That's the third time you are mentioning 'tiny' in less than two seconds!" Wilfred said, laughing out loud.

"Oh my! I want it so badly!" I said laughing hysterically.

Wilfred picked one off the hanger and handed it out to me, I didn't even bother collecting it from him.

"No, I want the tiniest one!" I said, pointing at the smallest one on the line.

"Dicks that fit into that are the rarely small dicks. Are you sure this will fit?" he asked, placing it in my hands.

I smirked as I ran my fingers over it. This cage is really small and Wilfred may be right.

"Don't worry, I'll force his dick in!"

"Damn!" Wilfred puffed and shook his head. "You are quite an interesting person, Martha."

"I know!" I replied, giggling.

I happily spent the money, knowing it will bring peace to Annabel.

Now that I have all those tools loaded in my car, I zoomed off to their house. Whether Micheal is at home or not, I can help myself in.

It took some twenty-five minutes for me to arrive at their home. There was hardly any traffic on the road.

The chastity cage, the blindfold, ropes and chain are the first things I will need. I tucked them into my bag, took a deep breath, walked to the door, opened it with the key and turned the doorknob.

As my steps clicked on the floor as I walked in, I heard him call from the passageway leading to their bedroom;

"Annabel?"

CHAPTER 3 – NO, IT'S NOT ANNABEL

I walked in without responding to his inquisition.

Eyes — red, hair — scattered, he stood facing me, bare-chested.

This is the maniac making life difficult for my sister. I was resolute on my purpose and ready to take him down.

His torso heaved rapidly and he looked confused. He slanted his head and scanned me from head to toe. And back up.

"Annabel?"

Damn! This dude is wasted! I know Anna and I have a resemblance, and placed side by side, you can easily tell we are siblings, but we aren't twins! We are not identical twins. Anyone in his right mind shouldn't mistake us for twins, not even for someone who knows both of us. I came prepared for combat, but obviously, there was no need for that. He is making it very easy for me.

He continued to look stunned, head slanted still and narrowing his gaze on me like he was trying to fix a bug.

"Annabel?"

I dropped the bag and closed up on him, yanked the brown tracksuit trousers down and reached for his balls. His scrotum is bigger than the one I tortured at G4, but not bigger than my hands, which I wrapped around it swiftly. Just one thing was left, — to squeeze!

"No, it's not Annabel, you waisted bastard!" I said as I squeezed his scrotum. I didn't expect what happened next;

He screamed extremely loud!

So loud I was scared and almost let go of the hold on his scrotum.

This is not my first time grabbing men by the balls. I know, it's always painful. Always. But for all the times I've done it, this is the most childish or emotional outburst I ever got. I mean, I still did this to someone just a few hours ago and he cried but didn't pull the roof down. Micheal wanted to pull the roof down with his scream.

All within seconds, within ten seconds, his head is hanging low, and lower as each second ticked afterwards. It's a big house they live in, but I hoped their neighbours wouldn't be knocking on the door in response to his 'alarm.'

Is this the man Annabel ran away from? Muscular and broad-chested, yes, but crying like a wimp already? *Pfffttt!!.*

This is going to be fun, and I need to place a mouth gag on him as soon as possible, but not until I have him shackled. The redness of his eyes is unusual and I wouldn't leave a loophole that could tilt the situation against me. You can never trust someone who is high on dope.

I clamped my thumb around the base of his dick and refreshed my hold on his balls. They are big!

Perhaps that's why he feels so much pain? I'm guessing the bigger the balls, the bigger the pain. Good for me, and good for him too.

Good for Anna, good for us all.

He held my knees to keep him from collapsing to the floor, and for doing that, I squeezed his balls!

He screamed again. "Pleaseeeeeeeee, pleaseeeeeeeee..." he began to cry.

"Don't touch me!" I said to him, slowly, clearly. "Don't touch me."

Instantly, he took his hands off my knee and wobbled. Just like that, his training started.

Dragging him by his balls, I walked to the spot where I dropped my bag, picked it and then approached the couch. I sat down, holding his balls in my hands. Without being told to, he went on his knees.

This was just too easy. He didn't attempt to fight back at all. Couldn't lift a finger. All he could do was scream, which I was now getting used to since I wouldn't allow that to stop me.

His left shoulder brushed against my leg, and I squeezed his balls again. He responded with a loud cry but quickly learnt to not let his body touch mine.

"M... Martha..."

"Ah, you are getting back to your senses now?"

While my right hand held his balls in a very tight fist, I pinched his nipples with my left hand. I had achieved my purpose of having him subdued, but I could as well be naughty and have fun with this.

"Martha, pleaseeee..."

The more I Inflict pain on him, the more the substances wear out and the more he gets back to his senses.

"Martha..."

"Don't 'Martha' me. Shut up!" I squeezed his balls again. He groaned and lost form more.

Pulses from the trembling of his thighs flowed to my arm. He was really in pain, not only could I see it, but I could also feel it.

The goal is to squeeze the life out of him, so I will continue to turn a deaf ear to his cries and pleadings. Men crying? That's something I'm well accustomed with. I love it.

His chest heaved rapidly now, and his breathing was laboured. Both his inhalation and exhalation were with grunts and groans. And he began to sweat too, though the weather wasn't hot, the weather around his balls was.

His grunts reduced, signalling to me that he needs some more pain, so I squeezed again. Very hard this time.

It was like he wanted to run mad. Pulling his hairs, hitting his thighs, biting his lips.

I relaxed the hold a bit after noticing shortness of breath. You will still faint, but not yet. Pain first.

"I want you naked, Micheal. Remove your trousers."

I didn't have to say it twice. He didn't even bother to check to be sure if he heard me correctly. He just pulled the tracksuit trousers off, instantly, and took a few moments to breathe.

His chest pulsed with laboured breathing. Except for being an idiot, he has a fine body. I did enjoy watching that. That chest, rising and falling. And of course, I stared at his whole lower body now. I liked him naked.

We are several minutes into this now and felt deeply satisfied as I watched tears run down his face. The tears seemed to replace the screams, as that took less energy. He didn't have enough energy left to scream.

Gradually, he got weaker under my hold. I'd need someone to research if there is a connection between the lungs and the scrotum of a man, because I always notice a connection. They find it difficult to breathe when I squeeze ther balls!

I've got a lot of plans for Micheal, and I am barely scratching the surface. I was ready to go deeper and hasten things up.

With a mean resolve, I squeezed his balls very tightly, as tightly as possible. He groaned with a deep voice and shed tears profusely. There was no one around to caution me, so he was at my mercy.

His head dropped to the floor and so did his hands. This was it, he was giving up. The only thing he managed to do now was breathe until it looked like he passed out. This is the moment I've been waiting for.

I took the small chastity cage out of the bag and tried to wear it on his dick.

The cage was too small for his dick! Wilfred was right. I should have picked a bigger one. I made a mistake, but no problem, like I told Wilfred, I will force his dick in!

The only part of him that remained active was his chest—rising and falling. No other part, no fighting back, no hindrances at all.

It took four attempts to successfully lock his dick in the micro cage. I wore the remote control shock ring on his scrotum and smiled. It's one of the first toys I bought at the dungeon and it works wonders. He won't believe this when he wakes up.

I wore the leashed dog collar on his neck too.

So, here is my sister's maniac husband, naked, collared, and locked in a chastity cage. The first night. More accurately, within the first hour, I had achieved this much.

My phone rang. It was Annabel.

"I'm sorry I'm calling so soon, Martha. I just can't help it. Do you need help? Should I call the police?"

I stared at Micheal's body and laughed.

"Damn, Martha. Crazy girl. How is he? Now that I know you are safe."

"Micheal? I'm waiting for him to get back up, he seems to have passed out temporarily."

She wanted to hold the laughter back, but she couldn't.

"Passed out?"

"Yes. And he is naked too. And I have locked his dick in a cage, wore a collar around his neck, you know, stuff like that."

"Oh my God!"

Annabel couldn't believe it. She thought I was joking. It was another superwoman moment for me and I pranced over my prey.

"Could you send a pic, I can't imagine."

"Hold on a sec..."

I took a picture of Micheal's naked body lying on the floor and sent it to her.

"Ohhhh my god! I can't believe this!"

She bounced and screamed on the phone. Rambling and merging words and half sentences.

"What the fuck! Wow!"

"Sweetheart, I'm still kinda busy. I want to tie him up with ropes now, and some other stuff. We'll talk later. But now, you know I'm safe."

"Wow! Okay, Martha. Wow."

She continued with 'Wow, wow," like the siren of an ambulance. I ended the call. Her joy knows no bounds.

Since Micheal began to toe the wayward path, he had laid hands on Annabel twice, and that broke my heart. To have him subdued gladdens my heart. He can't keep blaming his misbehaviour on substances he is unwilling to quit taking. I will ensure I put an end to it.

He rolled to his side and then noticed there was something around his neck. The collar.

He ran his fingers on it and opened his eyes, expressing his surprise. He traced the chain leash with his eyes.

"Welcome back, Micheal," I said to him. The tears had dried up on his face, but he still looked pitiful.

His hands and lips trembled as he looked into my eyes, afraid. Very afraid.

"Martha," he said, very softly and fearfully.

The remote was in my hand already, on and ready to help me with his training.

Bzzzzzzzzzzz!!

He groaned in response to the shock and pulled his knees to his chest.

"Goddess Martha! It's Goddess Martha."

His heart heaved rapidly again and he could no longer look into my eyes. *I just want to train you into a submissive husband, not make you scared of living,* I said in my mind, not uttering the words.

"Common, don't be shy. Try again."

"Goddess Martha," he said, with a broken breath.

"Yep! That's it. This is a good start."

He looked around and saw that it was just the two of us, still confused though, trying to make sense of how Annabel running out of the house led to him naked at my feet. But that shouldn't be difficult to figure out.

"Get on your knees, Micheal."

People learn very fast when you apply the right methods. Micheal is coming across easier than I thought. He got on his knees immediately, with his hands clasped behind him, head bowed.

Like seriously! "Are you a submissive?" I asked, curiously.

He looked up blank, having no idea what that means.

"A submissive is an obedient man who likes to do as Goddess says. Are you a submissive?"

He stared at the remote in my hand and looked back at me.

"Yes, Goddess, I am a submissive."

Bzzzzzzzzzzzzz!!

Just to remind him of the power I still have over him, I pressed the button again and sent shock waves into his balls.

He looked too weak to take on my next lessons, so I cuffed his hands, cuffed his legs, and bridged both cuffs with a rope tie. This way, he would be largely immobile.

"Calm down, Micheal," I said to him out of pity. He was looking too lost and scared for my likening.

I went into the kitchen to get us something to eat. There were some haddock stocked in the fridge, so I decided to make Fish and Chips.

I returned to the room with a full plate for him, to replenish his strength. I served my plate too, but I wasn't ready to eat just yet.

"Here, Micheal," I said to him as I dropped the plate on the floor. "Oops, sorry."

How would he eat being tied up like that? Amused, I untied the rope and removed the cuffs. But the collar and chastity cage remains. Those won't come in the way of his dinner.

He drank water first. Half of the cup I set before him. I cackled. *This guy has suffered today.*

His hand trembled and the potato chip fell off the fork.

"Use the fork properly, Micheal."

He pierced two pieces of fried potato chips and took a bite. Even his lips trembled. After his first three bites, he began to devour the food like a hungry lion. Strength was returning to his body. I admired what I was turning him to and the next thing I see, the plate is empty.

"Is that enough? Or you want more?"

"It's enough, Goddess, thank you."

Haha. I puffed. He sounded so sweet and respectful.

"This is the Micheal I used to know. Where did the maniac that beats and throws things at my sister come from? What happened to you, Micheal?" I asked genuinely, holding the ring shocker remote well though, I could need to push the button at any time.

He looked genuinely sorry. Now he knows what brought his present predicament upon him.

"Look at me and talk to me, Micheal."

Words were heavy on his lips and he fumbled at making coherent statements.

"I'm sorry, Goddess."

That was good to hear, but I wanted more. I wanted to know what pushed him to the edge.

Bzzzzzzzzz!!

He groaned. "Goddess, pleaseeee"

I ran my fingers in his hair like a little boy. "Calm down, boy, calm down. I'm only playing with you now."

Bzzzzzzzzz!!

"Being sober is not enough. This is the Martha Inquisition. I need answers. What happened to you, Micheal?"

The mumbo jumbo that followed cracked me up, though I tried not to laugh. He overworked himself trying to make sure there's no reason for me to push the button again. What he didn't know is that I don't need a reason! I will push the damn button anytime I feel like. Welcome to femdom, gentleman.

From all the rubbish and half statements he mumbled, the facts began to come out.

"It takes control of me, and sometimes I just love that feeling."

Aha! That's key.

"So, Micheal, you love to be controlled?"

"Err, that's not exactly what I'm saying..."

Bzzzzzzzzzzzzz!!

"You consume things that make you lose control, and you enjoy the 'high' it gives you, so what exactly are you saying, Micheal, do you like to be controlled?"

"Yes, Goddess, I like to be controlled."

"Aha! Better. That is it. Say it again."

"I love to be controlled, Goddess."

"Does that mean you love what I'm doing to you right now?"

"Yes, Goddess."

"Do you know what that collar around your neck signifies?"

He shook his head.

Bzzzzzzzzz!!

"Because I am a dog?"

"You are a dog. Yes. But try again."

"Wait," I said to him, "Go on all fours, like a dog."

He assumed the position, and I loved it. I remembered the butt-plugs. I took one out and lubed it.

T-h-a-u!!

I smacked his ass and poured some lube on his asshole. This is getting very interesting now, for me, and for him, seeing his pre-cum leaking out of the tip of the micro chastity cage.

"You love this, don't you?"

"Yes, Goddess, I love it."

For the fear of having his balls shocked, he answered anything that sounded like a question, even when it is rhetorical and I'm not expecting an answer.

Virgin asshole! I will have fun popping his cherry!

I slowly pushed the buttplug in against the resistance of his anal sphincter that refused to open. He grunted a little as the plug popped in.

"So, what does the collar around you neck signify? Try again"

"Because I am your pet?"

"Brilliant, that's closer."

He tried a few guesses around that, but I'm not about to waste time on that lesson.

"I am turning you into a slave, Micheal. That's what the collar signifies. You are now my slave. And Annabel's!"

"Yes, Goddess!"

"Good boy. Now confess that you are my slave."

"I am your slave, Goddess Martha."

It was a proud moment for me.

"Ewww, why are you leaking so much, lick that now. Clean it up."

Yet on all fours, he lowered his head and licked his precum off the floor.

"I want to eat my dinner now. Will you be my human table, Micheal?"

Bzzzzzzzzzzzz!!

"Yes, Goddess! Yes, Goddess."

He screamed. Not that he was slow to respond. I was going to push the button anyway, whether he answered promptly or not.

He moved closer, giving me his back to use, unto which I placed my plate of Fish and Chips. Life can be very interesting with men — when you subdue them.

Dinner tasted better in my mouth than it should have, than

usual. Dinner tastes better when you eat it on the bare back of a naked submissive man. Both my taste buds and my pussy were excited. The thrill is indescribable.

My phone rang again, and instinctively, I knew it must be Annabel. It was her.

"I'm going to bed, just want to check on you again to be sure you are okay. Are you?"

"Anna," I began, proudly, "I am eating Fish and Chips on Micheal's back. He is serving as my human table. Yes, I am ok."

"What!" Annabel gasped.

Of course, I expected that sort of reaction from her. "You are doing what, Martha?"

"Micheal is naked on all fours like a dog, and I am eating dinner on his back," I said slowly and casually.

"Martha, you are crazy!"

She ended the voice call and switched to a video call immediately.

"Here he is. Say hi, Micheal."

I focused the phone on his face, then on his shoulder and back. To satisfy her curiosity, I stood up so the camera could capture the whole display. Annabel resumed screaming 'Wow' like a siren.

I lowered the camera and closed in on his dripping penis.

"What's that? You padlocked his dick, Martha!"

"A cage. A chastity cage. That will help to keep his masculinity in check."

"Wow!"

"Sweetheart, will you go to bed now so I can continue with my dinner?"

We both laughed hard.

"Micheal is a good guy after all," I said to Annabel. "He made some confessions to me. He only went astray because of a need, and that need is being met right now, by a better and healthier mechanism. He's never going astray again. Right? Slave?"

"Yes, Goddess!" he screamed following a light push on the shock button.

"He just called you Goddess! Like the guy at G4!" Annabel blurted, laughing widely.

"Ain't I a Goddess?" I asked, laughing too.

We had fun chatting over him, and Annabel would just go on and on staring at her phone screen, amazed at what I had turned her husband to, the first night. The very first night! I know. I am bad like that.

CHAPTER 4 – DOMESTICATION

Just so I could sleep well, without the fear of a revolt from him, I tied him up before we went to bed. I cuffed his hands, cuffed his legs and bridged the cuffs with a rope. Then I wore the blindfold on him. And yet that wasn't all. The chain. The big D-ring chain.

I tied his ankles together with it and tethered the other end to the window. He looked pitiable, but I felt safe — with the shock ring remote beside me still.

It took him a long time to get used to the predicament bondage, which led to him sleeping late, hours after I was fast asleep.

When I woke up, he was the first thing on my mind.

I rolled on the bed and stared at him. He slept like a baby! I wondered how he eventually got comfortable. I wouldn't have been surprised if I woke to see that he didn't sleep all night.

I got into the bathroom and washed my body. It would be my first full day with him and the first full day of training.

Till I got in a sexy dress and smelled nice from cologne, he was still sleeping. I contemplated waking him up with a shock but changed my mind. *No, Martha, be nice for once.*

I was about to step out into the kitchen when I heard the rattling noise of the chain on the floor. I flipped my hair and turned backwards. Micheal. He's awake.

"Good morning, Goddess."

Whew, that sounded so natural. I walked closer to him as he raised his head and stared back at me. No animosity in his facial expression. No acrimony. No bitterness. He looked unto me like a chic would to the mother hen. I hunkered low and he placed his head on my laps.

Bzzzzzz!!

He grunted and placed his head back on my thighs.

"Yeah, good morning, slave."

I loosed the chain tether on the window and retreated to the bed. Holding on to the leash, I stretched my right leg to his face.

"Suck my toes, slave."

Slowly and respectfully, he held my foot and placed my big toe in his mouth and began to suck. For a first-timer, he made a good attempt at it. From the big toe, he moved to the rest of the toes, one by one, sucking hard on them.

"Open your mouth as wide as it can go."

I shoved my foot into his mouth. He gagged and began to salivate.

"Tasty, right?"

"Yeah, slurp on it."

He followed my instructions and worshipped my foot religiously. I then raised the left foot also and had him repeat the rituals.

Placing my feet together, my big toes were side by side.

"My big toes, Micheal, give them a blow job."

Like a slut, he slurped on my toes. Oh my, I got wet. My left hand found its way unto my clit, rubbing slowly, tenderly.

"You are such a cute dog, Micheal."

With renewed passion, like my words just encouraged him, he relaunched at my toes and gave all ten toes blowjobs.

"Moan, bitch, show me how you are enjoying it. Worship me, Micheal."

He briefly inhaled the smell of my toes and resumed slurping on them and moaning, chanting "Goddess, Goddess."

"Now let's do the soles. Make love to the soles of my feet."

All I could now see was the outline of his face and the hair on his head. His face disappeared behind the soles of my feet,

Why allow vices to make a man a maniac when he can be this useful when controlled?

I didn't foresee it, but the sweet sensations from the feet worship stimulating me to touch myself ended up driving me to an orgasm. I fell back on the bed and rested my feet on his face as he quickly lay his back on the ground to present his face as a receptacle for my feet.

When I got back on my ass, I stared squarely at him, with the remote in my hand.

"This must be what you were looking for, right, Micheal?"

"Yes, Goddess."

"You love to be dominated?"

"Yes, Goddess."

Bzzzzzzzzz!!

He groaned and kissed my feet. *Damn. This dude is a natural.*

"I'm going to make a decent slave out of you, Micheal. Come. We will start with you cleaning the house."

I held the leash and on all fours, he crawled to the vacuum cleaner and stared upwards at me.

"You can stand up."

He was very docile, seeking my attention before he does anything. Following him around as his instructor, he vacuumed the entire house, and afterwards dusted the furniture, with me smacking and grabbing his rigid butt cheeks as he did.

"You have been a good boy this morning. Goddess wants to reward you, are you happy about that?"

"Yes, Goddess, thank you, Goddess," he replied, light sparkling on his face.

"Would you like to cum? Goddess wants to play with your John Thomas."

He quirked his lips in a half-smile.

"Yes, Goddess."

"Alright then, the cage comes off!"

Reaching for the key of the chastity cage brought smiles on his face. He glowed as I unlocked and removed the cage.

*Ugggggh*hh, he heaved a sigh. I giggled.

"Was it uncomfortable?"

"Very! And even painful."

"Sorry. It's way too small for your big dick. But I like it."

Erection. His dick grew wide and long instantly, and he looked away from me, being ashamed of himself, which I liked.

"Micheal, bring your big pee-pee to Goddess, and let her play with it."

He shyly placed his dick in my hands and I rubbed it.

For a moment, the earlier ordeal flashed in his mind and he retracted. That experience must have been traumatic for him.

"Calm down, slave, not this time," I assured him. He relaxed again.

I lubed his dick and formed a ring around it with my thumbs and index fingers and jelqed it downwards. He dripped precum.

"Naughty boy," I commented, to make him shyer.

I lifted my fingers to his mouth and made him lick his precum off, then resumed milking him again. His dick throbbed in my hands.

His thighs started trembling and he moaned. I paused for a while. He looked helpless and desperate for my touch.

"Beg me."

"Please touch my dick, Goddess, he said, looking away shyly.

I resumed slowly stroking his dick and he moaned softly. His breaths shortened as I picked up pace with it. He moaned louder.

Should I ruin his orgasm? No. Martha, No.

He bent slightly forward as I stroke his hard dick, moaning louder until he cummed and blew his load on my feet.

"Lick that up, slave. Eat your cum."

He bowed on my feet and licked his cum off my feet. He was grateful.

"What do you say to Goddess for letting you cum?"

"Thank you, Goddess. He said and bowed."

"No worries. Now Goddess is gonna lock your dick back in the cage." I stretched my hands forward.

He sighed and dropped his dick in my hands. It was still a bit pumped and would in no way fit back into that micro cage like that. I needed it to shrink back to its natural minimum.

Bzzzzzzzzzzzzzz!!

He fell forward on my thighs, hugging my leg and breathing hard.

"Sorry darling, I need your dick to shrink, that's why. Goddess wants your dick to suffer in the cage."

Bzzzzzzzzzzzzzz!!

I held it in my hands again, and now it was totally flaccid, but not small enough for the cage and I'd still have to force it.

It took just two attempts this time to force his dick into the micro cage. I was getting better at it. I clicked the padlock shut and puffed. "Haha, here we go!"

"Won't you thank me for locking your dick in an undersized cage?" I said, laughing at and mocking him.

"Thank you, Goddess, for locking my cock in the cage."

"Are you sure? Slave, you aren't looking happy about that."

He forced a smile on his face and thanked me again. The smile was fake, but I liked it.

I took him out to the car, naked still, to carry the rest of the things I left in the car. Luckily for him, it wasn't busy outside, though there was the chance that anyone could have seen us in the garage.

"It's time for the next step in your training. Kneel away from me, head on the floor, ass up in the air."

"Spread your legs," I said to him as I kicked him. "Yes, like that."

"Now hold your ass cheeks and spread them apart."

I plopped out the buttplug and watched his asshole flicker.

T-h-a-u!!

I spanked his asshole.

Bzzzzzzzzzzzz!!

"That's for falling out of position. I want you to be a disciplined slave, Micheal. Stay in the position I put you. Don't flinch."

"Yes, Goddess."

"Now, let's try again."

T-h-a-u!!

I landed another stroke directly on his anal ring. He held on to his ass cheeks and spread them apart, despite the pain. He cried.

"Good job, slave. Good job."

This is the hyperactivity he wants that led him to abusive substances. I'm only replacing it with sadistic activities, so, there's no need to pity him. I am helping him, I muttered to myself.Watching his asshole redden and swell, I needed to convince myself to continue enjoying inflicting pain on him.

The tears came back. He cried and sobbed like a baby, begging me, but remaining in the spanking position.

T-h-a-u!! T-h-a-u!!
T-h-a-u!! T-h-a-u!!
T-h-a-u!! T-h-a-u!!

He shed tears profusely and begged. His asshole blazed red like the sun and he shrieked as I traced my fingers on the ring.

"Take your hands off your ass cheeks, let's rip those apart."

W-h-a-c-k!! W-h-a-c-k!!

He cried still, but apparently, he had just witnessed something worse, so this must have felt better, though yet painful.

W-h-a-c-k!! W-h-a-c-k!!

W-h-a-c-k!! W-h-a-c-k!!

W-h-a-c-k!! W-h-a-c-k!!

W-h-a-c-k!! W-h-a-c-k!!

W-h-a-c-k!! W-h-a-c-k!!

W-h-a-c-k!! W-h-a-c-k!!

To my utmost surprise, I checked his groin and found precum drooling out of the tip of his penis.

"Ha, Micheal, you are enjoying this!"

W-h-a-c-k!! W-h-a-c-k!!

W-h-a-c-k!! W-h-a-c-k!!

W-h-a-c-k!! W-h-a-c-k!!

W-h-a-c-k!! W-h-a-c-k!!

"You are a masochist!"

W-h-a-c-k!! W-h-a-c-k!!

W-h-a-c-k!! W-h-a-c-k!!

W-h-a-c-k!! W-h-a-c-k!!
W-h-a-c-k!! W-h-a-c-k!!

"And I am a sadist."

W-h-a-c-k!! W-h-a-c-k!!
W-h-a-c-k!! W-h-a-c-k!!

W-h-a-c-k!! W-h-a-c-k!!
W-h-a-c-k!! W-h-a-c-k!!

"Two can play this game!"

W-h-a-c-k!! W-h-a-c-k!!
W-h-a-c-k!! W-h-a-c-k!!

W-h-a-c-k!! W-h-a-c-k!!
W-h-a-c-k!! W-h-a-c-k!!

The more I tore his ass apart with the cane, the more precum oozed out of the tip of his penis. I can bet if his dick wasn't caged, it would be rock-hard now.

Welts drew all over his ass in all directions, but he remained in position, even when I would have understood if he fell off.

I lit a bunch of five candles and held it over his back.

He yelped as the first drops landed on his back, then responded with low grunts as I spread the hot wax all over his back up to his shoulders.

I noticed he takes pain on other parts of his body better than he does on his balls, and I can tell why that is; size. He has big balls.

"Turn around, slave."

He lay on his back and held his limbs up like a dog. The hot wax drops were more painful on his chest, stomach and abdomen than they were on his back.

I left him there and went into the kitchen to prepare breakfast. Roasted Lemon Chicken. It took an hour and a half for the oven to get this done, and Micheal had all that time to rest, lay on the floor and play with his leash. He was finding peace in servitude.

The chicken was big enough for us both, with Yogurt to go along with it.

I came into the room with a tray bearing the Roasted Lemon Chicken, well perfumed with garlic, wine and lemons.

Micheal remained submissive on the floor as I began to shred the chicken into my mouth.

"Hey, dog, take this!" I cut a small piece of chicken and dropped it on the floor beside my feet. He got back on all fours and picked it up with his mouth.

I held another piece up in the air and had him bite it off my hand without lifting any of his four dog legs off the floor.

I threw another piece towards the door. Micheal crawled there, picked it up with his teeth and crawled up, lifting his head to show me the piece.

"Eat," I commanded. He was loving the dog games, I could tell. This guy just wanted some action in his life, and now he's getting it.

I chewed a piece of chicken and spewed the mashed up mouthful on the floor. He crawled towards it and looked up at me.

"Eat," I ordered.

He lowered his head and picked it up and ate it, not showing me any irritation. He seemed to like it, or perhaps, maybe he just wanted to impress me. Whichever it was, that encouraged me to do more.

I chewed more mouthfuls and spat them on the floor. Like a hungry dog, he crawled around and ate them all.

I poured some yoghurt on the floor and watched him slurp on that too. It was fun for us both.

"Table," I said to him, and he already knew what that means. He stayed on all fours and presented his flat back to me, unto which I dropped the tray and ate my breakfast. When I was done, I gave him the leftover, which he gladly ate. He seemed to be having a good time with me.

Shortly before noon, I got sleepy and decided to take a nap. After about two hours, I was about to wake.

I felt a warm towel dabbing my toes gently as gentle hands massaged the soles of my feet. I woke up to find Micheal ministering to me. It wasn't a towel, it was his tongue.

Gosh! I didn't instruct him to do that, but he used his initiative to figure out that would make me happy.

"What a great slave you are, Micheal!"

Feeling shy, he tried to hide his smile, but I saw it. He was glad I loved it. I began to notice the more I dominate him, the more subservient he becomes, actively trying to please me.

I led him by the leash to the bathroom and dumped my panties and clothes from the previous day on the floor for him to hand wash.

"Start with my panties, slave. Sniff it."

As though he just won a lottery, his face lightened up and he excitedly held my panties to his nose.

"You like the smell?"

"Yes, Goddess."

"Enjoy it then. You have been a good slave."

For about five minutes, I watched him sniff my panties so hard, it made me chuckle.

"Lick it now."

There was a light stain on the crotch which he dissolved with his saliva and swallowed.

W-h-a-c-k!!

I slapped him and ordered him to start washing with soap. Again, excitedly, he began with the task. Domination. This was all he needed to bring balance into his life.

The lactose had found its way through my gut and a pocket of rectal air was beating against my anus from the inside.

"Micheal, I want to fart in your nose!"

"Yes, Goddess," he said and raised his face.

Gosh. How can you be so docile? Sweeeeeeeet!

I lifted my dress and sat my bare ass on his face, pulling my ass cheeks apart.

FFrrummmmmmmpp!!

I ripped a hot smelly fart right into his nostrils.

"Sniff sniff, piggy piggy!"

He inhaled my fart into his nose and got high on it.

"I guess this is the right substance for you, Micheal?" I giggled.

"Yes, Goddess" he answered promptly.

He finished washing and as we got back into the room, Annabel called. On video. There was no need to ask if I'm safe again. She knows I am. She sees I am.

"Micheal, I want you to apologize to Annabel for your bad behaviour," I said to him while he got on all fours.

"I'm sorry, Annabel," he said, looking into the phone camera.

I tucked the phone in between the mattress and the bed so he and Annabel could stare at each other while I administer some discipline to his ass.

W-h-a-c-k!! W-h-a-c-k!!

I caned his ass. "She can't hear you. Speak louder."

"I am sorry, Annabel!" he screamed.

W-h-a-c-k!! W-h-a-c-k!!

W-h-a-c-k!! W-h-a-c-k!!

W-h-a-c-k!! W-h-a-c-k!!

W-h-a-c-k!! W-h-a-c-k!!

I caned him so hard he cried loud and Annabel was moved by his tears.

I took the phone and focused the camera on his ass as I administered more spanks.

W-h-a-c-k!! W-h-a-c-k!!

W-h-a-c-k!! W-h-a-c-k!!

W-h-a-c-k!! W-h-a-c-k!!

W-h-a-c-k!! W-h-a-c-k!!

"His ass is so red, soft and swollen now," I said as I ran my fingers over the welts on his ass.

"Is this a dream?" Annabel asked me.

"Don't doubt your sanity now, sweetheart. This is real," I said chuckling. "He has a confession to make, listen to him."

"Slave, tell your wife what you confessed to me yesterday about being dominated."

He looked into the phone camera.

"I told Goddess I like to be dominated," he said to Annabel.

She laughed so hard her eyes got watery. "Martha, what have you turned him into?"

I smacked his head. "Tell her what I have turned you into."

"A slave," he said, looking straight into the phone camera. "Goddess Martha has turned me into a slave."

"Now tell her the house chores you have done this morning."

"Goddess Martha made me vacuum clean the whole house and dust all furniture. She also made me hand wash her clothes."

"Wow. Really?"

"Yes, really, I am now an obedient slave. I do whatever I am ordered to do."

"Haha, that's my boy," I said, patting his head.

It was an information overload for Anna to process.

"You pulled it, Martha!"

"Yes, sweetie, I did."

I wanted him to entertain us some more, so I reached for the remote to the shock ring around his scrotum.

Bzzzzzzzzzzzz!!

"Do you want to bark for us, slave?"

Wuff!! Wuff!!

Bzzzzzzzzzzzzz!!

"Come on, dog, try harder."

The shock was all the motivation he needed. He thickened his voice and barked louder.

Wruff!! Wruff!! Wruff!!
Wruff!! Wruff!! Wruff!!

Annabel and I laughed hard.

"Will she feel safe with you from now on?" I said, spanking his ass once more.

"Yes, Goddess Annabel, you will feel safe with me."

"Oh My, he just called me Goddess!" Annabel yelled excitedly.

"Ain't you a Goddess," I asked, rhetorically, smiling.

CHAPTER 5 – A BIGGER CAGE

I made Sandwich with Cheddar Cheese for lunch. While I ate and enjoyed myself, it was impossible to not notice Micheal's discomfort. He could not bother me, and I tried to ignore also, for as long as I could.

The way he tried to distract himself from the discomfort amused me. Flapping his laps, beating his thighs, knocking the table... None of them worked.

"Slave, what's going on," I ask, not being able to hold off interfering anymore.

"Nothing, Goddess," he replied, with as much indifference as he could summon.

Micheal is now at the point where the only thing he wants to do is please me. He gets scared of making requests that might piss me off. This, I liked.

"Slave, talk to me," I insisted, being bothered for him now.

He stopped eating and fixed his gaze on the table, not wanting to look into my face directly.

"Goddess."

"Yes, slave, go on..."

His face flushed and his lips trembled. This sight of him makes my pussy tingle. Naked, collared, scared and talking to me with utmost reverence.

"I'm listening, talk to your Goddess."

"Goddess, It's about my penis."

That brought a big smile on my face. It's exactly what I guessed was wrong. If Wilfred was here now, he would be telling me 'I told you so.' I was stubborn, but that's just part of exploration, and it's fun.

"What is it about your penis?" I asked like I'm his mother and him, my little boy.

He took a deep breath, as though contemplating whether to go ahead and open up to mommy or shut the fuck up. But I was smiling at him now, and there was no cane in my hand, nor the remote to the shock ring. That's enough to encourage him to share his thoughts.

"Talk to me, my boy, what is it with your penis?"

"It is paining me, Goddess."

"Awww..." I feigned pity. "Your penis is paining you? Come. Come and show Goddess your penis."

He walked over shyly, with toned muscles, biceps and six-packs on his abdomen, but shy like a kitten, gazing lower as he dropped his caged dick into my hands — it was struggling to breathe!

No wonder he is in pains.

His dick was swelling against the cage like it wanted to escape. I rubbed my fingers on the folds piercing out on the sides of the cage. Precum dripped from the tip.

"How painful is it, slave"

"It is very painful, Goddess, I can't breathe."

"Awww!"

"So, what do you want Goddess to do for your penis?"

He knows I love to keep him locked and so can't dare ask to be released. His problem was not so much the cage, but the size, which Wilfred warned me off.

"Goddess, please," he said as humbly and softly as he could, "If there is a bigger cage, that would be better."

I smirked. I'm liking how this is going.

"So, in essence, you want a bigger cage?"

He nodded, "Yes, Goddess!"

"Guess what! Micheal," his face lightened up, "I have a bigger cage for you!"

"Thank you, Goddess!"

The rest of lunch was with impatience. He was so eager to get into a bigger cage that would allow his dick some comfort.

I imagined how he would feel when he gets to discover the twist in what I had for him.

After lunch, I made him carry the large carton, one of the items he offloaded from my car.

There were questions on his face.

"You asked for a bigger cage. Here it is!"

He smiled, being confused. He must be wondering how can this be the bigger cage.

"What is it, slave?"

He giggled. "This is not only bigger than my penis, it is bigger than my entire body."

Yep. That's the clue right there.

We opened the cartoon and there were steel bars everywhere. Bars bars bars. And screws.

Following the manual, I gave him instructions on which joints to screw on which, and halfway through coupling it, the truth revealed itself.

"Come on, slave, don't be sad," I said to him when he realized this was not a penis cage, rather, a body cage."

He got quiet, and the excitement on his face vanished.

"Is your penis still paining you?" I asked, jokingly.

"No, Goddess. Please. The cage is just fine. I don't need a bigger one."

I rolled on my side, laughing out loud. "Come on! Your penis is paining you and you will like a bigger cage. Don't change the story."

A smile found its way on his face again.

"You know you can't escape this."

"I should have kept quiet."

I laughed. "Even if you did, I brought this and would cage you in it anyway. It was gonna happen!"

He sighed. It looked magnificent when he got done coupling it. Black-polished steel. 6 Ft by 4 Ft.

"This is a lot of space, boy. Do you like it?"

"Yes, Goddess. I like it." – though he didn't.

"Where can we place it?" I asked, wanting to involve him in setting up his new home.

"What if we use the guest suite?" I asked. He almost passed out. Of course, that was a joke, but it did get to him. "Or would you like the living area?"

I enjoyed seeing his face wash with every horrible suggestion I made.

As expected, we ultimately settled for their large and expansive bedroom. From the door of the restroom to the east wall was just the appropriate space to contain the length of the cage.

I held his ears like a naughty boy and shoved him into the cage. He crawled out laughing. Who is playing with you?

Bzzzzzzzzzzz!!

He growled and crawled back in.

"You want a bigger cage. Now you have one. You should be happy," I taunted him.

"Crawl around and sniff the corners."

"Yep. We will place a dog bowl here, bones here," I pointed, as he crawled around in the metal cage, sniffing its corners as I instructed.

I grabbed the lube bottle, surgical hand gloves and the buttplug.

"Come here, doggy, lets play," I said to him, sitting on a stool at the entrance of the cage.

He faced away, head on the floor, ass in the air.

W-h-a-c-k!!

I smacked his ass. "Oh, how I love this rigid butt of yours, Micheal. It's time for your 'bitch' training."

I wore a pair of surgical gloves and applied an ample amount of lube on his asshole.

"Open your cunt, bitch!" I ordered as I smacked his ass. His frail attempts at opening his asshole were amusing. At most it puckered, and that was all.

I slid my index finger into his asshole. It gave way. The buttplug had cleared the way.

He grunted as I slid the entire length of my index finger in.

"Haha, bitch, your cunt is warm."

I twisted my finger inside and probed his man cunt with it. The warmth was charming.

I pulled it out until it was just the tip left and rammed the whole finger back in. I repeated this for like ten minutes. His grunts reduced.

In place of the index finger, I pushed my middle finger into his cunt. He grunted, reacting to the longer length. I pulled it out and drove it back in. Poured more lube and drove the finger back in.

W-h-a-c-k!!

"Spread your ass cheeks for me, bitch."

I picked up pace and began to fuck his man cunt with my middle finger. The grunts came back, but I was comfortable with that. They turned me on.

His buttcrack was now greasy and shiny. Sexy.

I stuck my index and middle fingers together and drove them both into his asshole. He grunted louder, but that didn't stop me. I went in until both fingers couldn't go in any further. Then I began to fuck his hole with both fingers. Fast. Rapid. Occasionally smacking his ass with my left hand.

W-h-a-c-k!!

"Roll your waist, slut."

He twisted and rolled his waist to the rhythm of my thrusts. Precum leaked out of the tip of his dick again.

"Slut!" I gasped.

W-h-a-c-k!!

"Yes, that's it. Roll your waist and moan for me, bitch. Say sweet things, moan for me."

Like a pro slut, he rolled his waist and moaned louder than before.

"Ohhh, yes, Goddess. Fuck me, Goddess.

Uhhhhhh, I love it, Goddess. This is so sweeeeet!"

I smacked and finger-fucked him rapidly to the point he could no longer talk but only groan.

"This is just the beginning, slave. I'm going to plunge a dildo into this warm hole of yours. Start liking to get fucked this way. You are a bitch."

We needed to try something else. I placed the back of my hand on my thigh and raised the two fingers with which I was fucking him up.

"Bitch, bounce your ass on my fingers. Ride my fingers like a hot vixen."

He spread his legs and gently descended his puckering asshole on my fingers. They slid in.

Like I instructed, slowly, he started bouncing his ass on my fingers.

"Damn. You will do so well on my strap-on."

He gagged as I shove both fingers in his mouth and made him suck them.

"Rest. We are going out shopping in the next hour."

◆ ◆ ◆

The Caucasian sales rep approached us after I beckoned to her.

"I'm having a problem with picking one of these for my pet. Which one do you think will fit better?"

"Your pet?" she asked.

"Yes, my pet, him," I replied, pointing at Micheal, who fidgeted and nervously looked away.

"Turn around, Micheal, let her see your ass," I return my gaze on the Caucasian lady, "Just to let you have an idea of what we are working with." I figured that would help her in helping me make a decision.

We could have shopped online, but that would skip the fun in humiliating him in a physical store.

The lady giggled and stared at his ass, and I grabbed both ass cheeks while she checked them out.

"Is he your sub?"

Wow, is she a d/s person also?

"Yes, he is," I excitedly replied.

"I have a sub too, and I make him wear girly things."

What a coincidence this is. I only wanted to humiliate Micheal, now I'm meeting someone interesting while at it.

"Do you fuck him? If you do, I'll recommend the crotchless panties. That will make his asshole available on demand."

"Oh gosh, we should be friends!"

"My pleasure!"

She took us to the next row and I see an array of colourful crotchless panties.

"Let's try this one on him."

Oh fuck, I'm loving this girl!

"Slave, take your trousers off!"

We can see other shoppers' heads above the rail on the other rows. We are not alone, but we are getting Micheal naked. This excited me so much.

It looked like he would prefer to sink into the ground to escape this, but that's not happening. He looked around and pulled his dark grey cashmere trousers off.

I'm glad that's all I allowed him to wear, I would have been embarrassed for letting him wear too much clothing and appear boring to this dominant sales girl.

The sight of the chastity cage delighted her.

"Whoosh! That's so small!"

"His dick?" I asked like I didn't know what she was referring to.

"No. The cage!"

"Ha, oh... Yeah, that's small."

"You are not a very nice Domme," she said to me, jokingly.

"Oh, dear, I'm not," I replied, laughing out loud.

"Can I touch it?"

"Of course, please, go ahead."

She reached her hand lower and jacked his dick towards herself. "Poor thing."

The first panties he tried on was an orange crotchless pantie with a silver ring on both sides. Such a flashy skimpy thing made him looked silly against the background of his muscular thighs.

"I like this. We are taking it."

We picked a total of ten panties in different colours.

"My bitch would like to thank you by humping your leg," I said to the lady, and she excitedly stepped a foot forward.

"Now doggy," I snapped my fingers.

Micheal shamefully crouched on her leg and humped her. We laughed so hard some other lady came around to see what was happening, which made his face to redden more, from shame.

"When will he cum?" she asked, after seven minutes of dry humping. He went on for another three minutes and still couldn't cum. The cage wouldn't allow him too.

"Please, let's give him some time. I'd like to see him cum," the lady says.

"Focus!" I say to Micheal. "Focus now and cum for Goddess."

That workes the magic. He banged his caged dick hard against her leg continuously until his semen poured on her feet.

"Oops, we're so sorry, he will clean it up," I said to the lady, giggling.

Micheal lowered his head and licked his cum off her feet.

"You have made my day," the lady said to me, while Micheal wore his trousers back.

"Just as you made mine," I replied.

I bought bangles, cheap makeup kit, a short dress, and a few other things, and we paid on Micheal's card.

His feet knocked against each other as we walked out of the store. Not only the Caucasian lady stared at us, but a few other shoppers who saw that little episode of ours did too.

I looked at his face, and it was just red. Red with shame, but obedient still to my will.

"A good slave has to be ready to serve at any place, at any time," I say to him as he sulked behind the steering. "Don't look so sad. You had fun. You cummed!"

He has been doing well with submitting in the house, but public humiliation ruffled his feathers, which is quite understandable.

Back at home, I was so eager to see him on the things we bought. He bathed and stood before me, his naked body a canvas for me to work on.

He wore the orange pantie again, with three pieces of bangles on both wrists.

He knelt before me and I applied a facial moisturizer on his face. Next was a primer, over his forehead, around his nose and on the rest of his face. It was evening already and we weren't going anywhere, but I couldn't think of something else we'd rather be doing. Not after we just bought all these beautiful things.

"When I'm done with you, Micheal, you will be a pretty girl. Your friends will be jealous of you," I taunted him, twisting his nipples.

"And the clamps are coming on these nipples. Remind me if I forget."

Next was applying the foundation. His face was blemish-free, so there was no need to use the concealer.

I added pink blushes to his cheeks and asked him to smile for me. He looked pretty. The transition from man to barbie was coming up fine. I applied his eyeshadow, eyeliner and finished up with a mascara that added length to his short lashes.

After lining his lip with a balm, the lip liner came on it, after which I applied red lipstick. I finished up with his face and stood him before the mirror.

"What do you see, Micheal, a pretty girl or a slut?"

"A pretty girl."

Oh, ok. I know what to do to get what I want. With the red lipstick, I wrote the word SLUT in block letters on his forehead.

"What do you see now?"

He smiled. He has to agree with me and see things my way to be happy.

"I see a slut, Goddess."

"Aha! Now you are seeing well."

We both had a good laugh.

"If you try to play smart with me, it will only get worse. You should have known that by now."

Following my instruction, he wore the short pink dress we bought and perfectly looked like a girl now. I found him irresistible and kept ogling his perky ass.

Should I fuck this ass now? Yes, I should.

I grabbed my strap-on dildo from my bag and asked him to kneel before me. He knew what was coming, and it scared him.

"Suck my dick, slut."

It must be his first time. He lowered his head and circled his lips around the strap-on dildo. My pussy got wet.

"Annabel should see this. You are good!"

Saliva drooled out his mouth as he slurped on my rubber dick. I held his head down and forced him to deep throat it. He gagged, as expected. Then I released the hold and he kept sucking hard on it.

There's no way I'd enjoy that so much that I would forget to fuck him. He seemed to work hard at it to hold the next step back. Pretty much a stupid logic.

If anything, that vigorous sucking action will only motivate me to fuck him hard. And that was about to happen.

"Micheal. Do you remember I told you I will enjoy popping your cherry?"

"I remember, Goddess."

"Now is the time. Give me your ass."

My heart skipped a beat. I am about to peg my sister's husband!

I poured an ample amount of lube on his virgin asshole. It pulsed in fear.

"It is well with your soul, Micheal, just relax."

"Relax. Relax. Relax."

I spoke calmly and popped the tip of the dildo into his ass. He grunted and stayed still.

Slowly, I pushed an inch in, waited a few seconds, then pushed another inch in.

"That's it, slut, you are doing well."

I pushed another inch in. Then another.

Micheal's virgin asshole consumed the six inches dildo. All of it.

I pulled outwards and in one slow move, I drove the entire six inches in at once.

I pulled out again and this time, I drove the six inches in faster than the first attempts. He reacted with low grunts.

"I can fuck you now, Micheal, just keep your ass up."

I smacked his ass and drove the strap-on dick balls deep into him. I started banging him on rapid mode.

He grunted louder and louder. Louder and louder.

Then the grunts slowly transitioned into groaning.

He groaned louder and louder. Louder and louder. And I smacked his ass.

"Bitch."

"Roll your waist."

You know, as the saying goes, what is worth doing at all is worth doing well. If he wants to be a slut, he's got to be a good slut for Goddess.

CHAPTER 6 – BROKEN

I showered in the bathroom – while standing on Micheal's back. Just having him helplessly bowing to my whims gives a great feeling. Subsequently, I watched him bathe, instructing him on where to wash first, like a little one.

I unlocked the chastity cage, just so he can breathe a little before what will be his longest night ever, in which he will sleep in two cages – a micro chastity cage and a big dog cage.

He doesn't always know what to expect, because I don't always reveal what comes next until I throw it in his face.

"You look happy, Micheal," I say to him, noticing the way he joyfully leaps around me.

Why? Before the bath, I removed the collar around his neck, and now that the chastity cage is off also, he feels free for the first time since my arrival. Stark naked, but having no item of bondage or humiliation on.

This won't last, he should know, but he doesn't seem to do.

He was all over me in the kitchen like a puppy. The collar is off his neck. The cage is off his dick. The shock ring is off his balls, and yet he is mine to command as I will.

"Micheal, lick the floor," I said to him.

He went on all fours and started mopping the spot with his tongue, the spot I just moved away from.

"You now worship the floor I walk on."

"Yes, Almighty Goddess," he says to me and resumes swiping his tongue, picking up dirt, but not minding stooping that low for my pleasure.

Micheal is broken.

Broken to my will, broken to my pleasure, broken to my lordship.

His enslavement is complete now, and I would start making plans to draft Annabel in.

We are having Bangers and Mash this evening, and as usual, I'm eating at the dining table while he eats at my feet. That was my plan. It changed.

"When she comes back, I'd like you to sniff Anabel's ass a lot. You will start with mine. Come now, Micheal."

I didn't repeat that. He left his meal instantly and crawled behind me with his head upturned under my ass which I lifted off the chair.

I spread my ass cheeks apart and descend it on his face. It was a paradise for him, as indicated by his dick that erected immediately and began to throb hard.

My ass cheeks went down on both sides of his ears, completely burying his head in my fat ass. I shifted my ass around on his face until I located the tip of his nose with my anus.

"Is that it?" I asked.

That must be it, since he couldn't talk, but he did raise his hand and gave me a thumbs-up sign. "Good boy," I muttered.

"Now, all you have to do is relax and breathe. Just relax and breathe."

His chest begins to rise and fall, lifting me up and down as I continued with dinner. I giggled.

"This is some nice sport, in so many ways. You get to sniff my sweet anus and do some weightlifting with your chest. You will look even more fit."

We weren't having conversations anymore, it was just me eating and talking. If he needed to respond to anything, it had to be with his hands.

Bup Bup Brrrrrrrrupp!!

"Yup! Sniff sniff, piggy piggy," I jovially say to him as I ripped a nasty fart into his nose.

I was impressed with his efforts. He drew my farts into his nose, inhaling fast, hard and deep. The onion gravy, butter and milk part of the meal must make my fart very smelly, but I can't know myself, since no traces of my farts escaped. Micheal was taking them all.

Fbruppppppp!! Brummmbbbb!!

FFrrummmmmmpp!!

My anus puckered on his nose and blasted a series of long nasty farts into his nose. He begins to sweat now but keeps working hard to please his Goddess.

I felt the tip of his nose drawing air out of my anus. The feeling of that excited me and I started getting wet. I don't know why most d/s activities turn me on.

Krrrrrrr Bhomppppppppppppppppppp!!

Damn! That was a bomb!

"Micheal, are you there? Are you still awake?"

He responded by raising a thumbs-up sign. I heaved a sigh of relief.

"Gosh. What a hard-working man you are."

Annabel calls me again.

"Sisterrrrrrrrrrrrrr!" she screams on the phone. That startled me a bit because I couldn't figure out what was exciting her.

"You seem to be having fun over there, you this naughty girl."

"Oh yes, I am. How did you know?" I chuckled. "I am sitting on

Micheal's face and ripping farts in his nose while eating dinner. Paradise has no better luxuries than this!"

"Martha! You are..."

"Farting in his nose. I am farting in your husband's nose!" I replied, laughing my ass out into Micheal's nose;

Brappppp! Brppppppppp! Brammbbbbbbbbbbbbbbbb!!

"Jeez! Martha!"

"Yeah, baby. You will enjoy him when you come back in here. I have broken him into an obedient dog. Anna, you owe me Two Hundred Million Pounds for my services!"

She and I laughed hard over the phone, and all through that, like a dedicated dog, my sister's husband keeps his nose up my anus and keeps sniffing.

"It's safe for you to come back home now. Micheal has no vices again. The only vice he has now is obeying orders!"

"Haha! Great job, Martha."

"I told you. I'm a pro at breaking men."

After I was done eating dinner and farting in his nose, he got back on his meal, with a sweaty face and a slightly bent nose.

"Everything is coming back on, slave. The collar. The cage. The ring. The plug. Everything."

The hairs on his body stood as goosebumps erupted. He was scared as fuck, but knelt at my feet, submitting his body, to do as I please with it.

I wore the shock ring back around the base of his balls and then forced his dick back into the micro chastity cage. He bowed as I wore the collar around his neck and for the next item, he bent forward away from me, raising his ass like a good slut.

The buttplug plopped in and I smacked his ass. "Good boy!"

I walked him into the cage like the pet dog that he now is, crawling on all fours. The plug shone in the middle of his ass.

I tied the leash on one of the bars of the cage and tossed a pillow in there to help him get a bit comfortable.

"Goodnight, slave."

"Goodnight, Goddess."

◆ ◆ ◆

Next morning at the dining table, all I needed to do was lift my bare ass off the chair and wink at him. Micheal left his meal and positioned himself behind my ass.

"Are you getting used to my ass now?"

"Yes, Goddess," he replied, his voice muffled into my ass.

"I want your mouth this morning, not your nose. Make love to my anus with your mouth and watch out for my farts. I want you swallowing them when I bless your mouth, Okay?"

"Yes, Goddess Martha."

I sat my weight in his face and balanced with the breakfast table.

"Tasty?"

He responded by humming. This dog was busy with my anus already.

"I want you to get used to the scent of anus. It's a beautiful thing to have your nose stuck on a beautiful woman's anus, isn't it?"

He didn't mind me much, he only workes hard on the task I gave him.

"Hold on a sec, I want to fart. Seal your lips around my anus!"

He stopped licking and wrapped his lips around my anus, waiting for my ass gas.

Bruuunnffffffffffffffff!!
Brubbb Bbfpffffffppppppp!!

I pumped his cheeks out with loud and long farts.

"Oops, it's so relieving to know you are there to catch that with your mouth.

This is exactly how you will be sniffing and eating Annabel's farts. If she calls to lay any complaint, I'd come here and beat you into a coma!"

He resumed french-kissing my asshole even after I was done eating and was merely drinking warm milk.

I led him to the living room where I wanted to watch some Sunday morning shows. He lay on the couch having his head at the spot I pointed to.

"You will have to work hard now, Micheal. I'm sitting on your face for a full hour, without any breaks."

He took a deep breath but still didn't look ready. I doubt if he could indeed get ready for such. I just sat on his chest first and had him heave me up and down with his respiration. I would advise any woman to do this on a muscular man, it's fun.

I couldn't do that for too long because of the noise in my stomach, some pockets of air were being dislodged lower down my colon.

"Another fart is coming already, my dear fart eater."

I slid my ass unto his face, and like a magnet draws a metal, his lips drew my anus to itself and wrapped around it.

"Don't worry," I said to him, seeing he only waited for the fart, "Lick and suck my ass. Whenever it comes out, it will be into your mouth still."

I dialled Annabel's Phone to remind her, in case she forgot.

"Two and a Half Men!" she said to me before I could say anything to her. I laughed.

It's our favourite show and we never miss it.

"And let me guess, Micheal is under your ass?"

"Yes."

"No. That can't be possible. Really?"

"I swear."

"Martha, since last night!"

"Of course, I allowed him to sleep. But now that he is awake and that I have crushed him to Zero and a Half Man, what else would he rather be doing?"

We gossipped ten minutes into the show before we suspended the call, after which my body focused on the pleasure Micheal's tongue was delivering to me underneath.

I not only find it erotic, but I also find it stress-relieving too. It's like a massage. The more he pressed his tongue against my bum-hole and licked and sucked it, the more relaxed I felt. I felt so relaxed I started feeling sleepy towards the end of the show.

My anus widened and hissed a fart into his mouth.

Psssssssssssss!!

I felt it blowing against his tongue which didn't retract though I was subjecting it to such a degrading thing.

"Annabel, he is looking forward to serving you like this."

She takes a deep breath. Seeing Micheal conquered has elated her heart so far, but she just has not been able to imagine herself in my place, degrading the love of her life in such a deplorable manner.

"You see how much he respects me now. If you want him to respect you in like manner, you have to allow him to serve you."

I began preparing her mind and convincing her of dominating him, not merely coming back home to live with a submissive husband. He has to keep submitting each day, and I won't always be around to receive that submission.

"I will give it a try, Martha."

"You will do it, Anna, there's no going back. It's fun, I promise."

She had to mentally agree she would dominate him and I promised to not only stay a few more days with them but always come check on them from time to time. After all, It's me who broke him into what he is now.

"When are you coming, Anna? We are waiting for you. I will prepare lunch for three."

She giggled.

"Alright love, I should come back between noon and 2 pm."

I playfully bounced my ass on his face and then asked him to shower. "Annabel is coming back home. Let's get you prepared."

◆ ◆ ◆

I laid the makeup kit, bangles, dress, chastity cage, collar and all the other toys I use on him o the table, while he bathed himself. Making him up will be easier now since I had already worked on his face before.

"Let's make up your ass first," I said to him as he knelt facing away from me, with his head on the floor and ass up in the air.

This will be intense, for Annabel's sake. I want her to see the extent to which her Micheal can go. I want the state in which she will find him do the speaking.

"This will be intense," I said to Micheal, as I rubbed oil on his ass, just to make it look for sexy for my sadistic mind. It's his wet naked body before me now, no article on him.

"You will need your strength. Save it. I don't want you crying," I said, tracing his anal sphincter with my fingers, "That's an order."

I picked the short cane and slid it longitudinally along his ass crack. His asshole flickered. He knew what was coming and how painful it would be.

"Are you ready, slave?"

"Yes, Goddess."

"Here we go. Contain yourself."

T-h-a-u!!

I flogged his asshole. There wasn't much time to start slow, so it was a hard stroke.

He didn't flinch, and that impressed me.

T-h-a-u!! T-h-a-u!!
T-h-a-u!! T-h-a-u!!

I went hard again and flogged him more, and yet, as if my words indeed programmed him, his still didn't flinch, and I was beginning to see the desired result on his asshole.

T-h-a-u!! T-h-a-u!!
T-h-a-u!! T-h-a-u!!

T-h-a-u!! T-h-a-u!!
T-h-a-u!! T-h-a-u!!

Now I'm hearing grunts though he yet remained in position.

T-h-a-u!! T-h-a-u!!
T-h-a-u!! T-h-a-u!!

T-h-a-u!! T-h-a-u!!
T-h-a-u!! T-h-a-u!!

I checked his face. He was shedding tears without making any sound. It moved me.

"That's it, let the pain flow through you."

Hard strokes directly on his asshole flamed it up, leaving it red and swollen. Then I moved on to the ass with a long cane.

I caned him very hard, so hard all he could now do was grunt and groan in agony. When the whole of his ass was covered in welts, I stopped. He shed tears profusely, but that was it. No noise, as I instructed.

His thighs trembled and he sobbed quietly. There was that nervousness caused by not knowing when the next stroke will land on his ass. Moving my palm over his butt cheeks, he yelped as I brushed the welts and swellings.

"Your ass is red and swollen now. When Annabel comes back, you will present this ass to her."

He recited some lines I taught him, and some moves too. His default position is to keep head bowed, hands behind his back and legs separated, making his genitals accessible.

I smiled at him and held my palm out.

"Goddess, please, can I say something?" he pleads with me, scared out of his bones.

I love this reverence he has for me. He is shaking and quaking on one spot just because he wants to speak with me.

"Go on, slave, I'm listening."

He stared at my hand and moved closer, then he placed his dick and balls on my hand, obeying first, before making his plea.

This to me is the height of submission. He is making me know that my will shall be done, even if I don't grant his supplication, which I know I won't grant.

His balls are the most sensitive part of his body, and that's what freaks him out. I can compare his reaction when I spank his asshole and when I torture his balls. Both are painful, but he can deal with one more than the order. Balls torture freaks him out, and that I can understand.

"Please, my ass is on fire but can I take the punishment on my balls there instead? Please," his lips twitched as he spoke, his eyeballs as red as his ass is.

I shook my head and scratched his chin. "I'm sorry sweetheart. I love playing with men's balls!"

He got super nervous as I held his scrotum in my hand and pressed to feel the balls. I wasn't inflicting any pain yet, but his mind was already suffering from what would follow.

I wished I could just do that for him, listen to his plea, oblige him and spare his balls, but that's not happening. *Would I ever pass on that chance? Not likely.* It's fast becoming a hobby for me, not just something I do to subdue men.

"I know you will be happy when I leave this place and go back to my house."

He managed to smile at my joke and act like it's not true. "I will keep showing up randomly though," I said, sticking my tongue out at him.

"Just relax, it will be painful, but you won't die. You will survive it."

I thought that would calm him down. It didn't. He raised his index finger again, signalling that he would like to say something, if I permit. I did.

"Are you going to make me pass out again like you did that other time?" he asks solemnly.

His facial expression was not that of anger or revolt, rather it was that of fear and reverence.

"I don't know. Should I make you faint?"

"No, no, please," he jumped in.

That humoured me and I laughed out loud while holding his scrotum in my hands. I would have begun to torture his genitals already, but I prefer to revel in his fear and agitation a bit longer. It's pleasing — staring into the eyes of someone who is so scared of what you can do to them. It's pleasing to stare into the eyes of someone who desperately needs your mercy. It's incredibly pleasing when you engage such a person in conversation and watch their lips tremble upon every word they try to speak.

"Why do you have big balls like that of a ram?"

He quirked his lips up in a smile and then stops halfway as I clutched his scrotum in my palm and displaced the balls around in the sac. He got scared, thought I was going to bust his balls.

"Were you a ram in your former life?"

He lets go and laughs out loud, and then stared at his balls as if to see if his balls were indeed as big as a ram's.

Gradually, he was calming down. Conversing with him soothed his nerves a little. We were connecting on some sort of friendship level, though just as between a superior and their employee. He liked it still because it made him feel better.

He has gone through a lot in my hands and is still about to go through some more torture. It just suddenly felt cool to at least put some smile on his face. If I have the power to make him cry, I should also have the power to make him laugh.

"You still haven't answered my question, Micheal. Were you a ram in your former life?"

He laughed out loud now. "I guess I was, Goddess."

CHAPTER 7 – ANNABEL

I squeezed his balls. Very hard.

His eyes popped out like that's what I squeezed. He kept his gaze steady on me. Looking deep into my eyes, looking for mercy. Mercy that he wouldn't find. Not now.

"Micheal," I called his name quietly while hurting him, "Micheal."

The frown on his face due to the pain got rougher, and soon afterwards, it turned to tears. I shook my head as I watch the first tears roll down his face.

"This looks familiar, Micheal," I say to him and he keeps looking at me still. "We've been here before."

At that place of tears and pain whilst his balls are in my hands? Yes. We've been there.

The calmness on his face disappeared, replaced by despair and fear. The fear of Martha. The fear of what I am capable of.

"Goddess," he said softly, looking into my eyes as he shed another tear, "Goddess."

I squeezed his balls harder, holding my gaze on him still. "Slave," I replied softly, jacking his balls up nearer to me and tightening my clasp on his balls, "Slave."

He and I are bonding through the pain I am causing him. It's becoming intense, but his cock is swelling, despite the pain. The hairs on his body are erecting too.

Ten minutes further into squeezing his scrotum, he loses the erection and his dick shrinks. It became even smaller than his pinkie.

With my other hand, I pinched the tip of his dick. He winced and sobbed. He wouldn't stop piercing into my soul with his eyes, searching for mercy.

His knees began to knock against each other and could no longer stand properly. He bent forward, dropping his head lower than his shoulder. I squeezed tighter. He winced. The G4 scenario is replaying itself like a movie I've watched before.

I had to hunker down with him as he lost balance and struggled to stay on one foot. The pressure on his balls became very threatening because he couldn't bear his own weight any more.

He laid quietly on the floor and did only one thing — sob.

He could hardly breathe, as though it were his lungs I was crushing, when in fact, it was his balls. This is no longer new to me.

After he stopped moving his limbs, and at that point of ultimate surrender, I stopped crushing his balls and wore the shock collar around it instead.

His cock was shrunk, so I wore the micro chastity cage on him while he just lay down there.

The next bondage article was the collar, which I wore around his neck, and since his swollen asshole had rested a bit, I shoved the buttplug in. He gasped as it popped in.

"Hey sissy, get up," I said to him.

It took him a few seconds before he coordinated himself and got on his feet, looking pitiful.

I patted his head and held him close to my heart. "You have suffered a lot today, but this is just half of it. I'm still going to fuck the hell out of you," I said to him, as softly as I could.

He held me tightly, drawing emotions out of me, comforting himself in the embrace. He didn't know I was holding the remote of the shock ring on his scrotum.

Bzzzzzzzzzzzz!!

He held me tightly and I held him back as I electrified his balls.

"Aww, my puppy!" I rubbed his head romantically. "Let's make you look like a beautiful girl!"

I applied makeup on his face and painted his lips red. I found one of Annabel's wigs in the wardrobe and wore it on his head to make his feminization more wholesome. He indeed looked like a girl. Then he wore the pretty pink dress and forced his feet into one of Annabel's high heels. I wore a panty on his ass and now his dressing was complete. I'm sure if I got him on the streets like this, someone would likely woo him.

I instructed him to catwalk around the house. He tripped and fell forward on his face on his first few attempts, but he kept getting back up and trying. After a while, he learnt to take the steps very slowly and avoid falling. He fell still, and I laughed hard at him. His feet are bigger than the heels, and that's a big problem.

I stared at him and mentally ticked off the points one by one.

Makeup. Dress. Chastity. Shock ring. Buttplug. Teary eyes. Bruised butt. Busted balls. Sore asshole.

All checked!

He clasped his hands behind him and stared at me from beneath his brow as I wore the strap-on. He still felt unexcited about getting fucked, though I had fucked him once already.

"I forgot to ask you, Micheal. How did you feel about losing your virginity to me?"

He smiled and looked away, being shy about it.

Annabel should come in at any moment from now, since she said between noon and 2 pm. Because I know I will be busy on Micheal, I left the door unlocked, since her key is with me. *Besides, would it not be nice if she comes in and sees me in action?*

I led him into the cage and stood by the door. Micheal's ass is sweet, and I want to take it again.

"Give me your ass, slave, doggy style!"

He went on his knees and elbows, head down, ass up, just the way I like it.

Staring at his bare ass, I'm reminded he has suffered a lot. His ass was a mess. Welts dashed in every direction. Welts and swellings. I popped the plug out of his asshole. It pulsed in and out like it was excited to see my strap-on.

I decide to go in gently this time, without smacking his ass.

In one steady and slow move, I drove the strap-on into his ass, balls deep.

"You're good at taking it now eh?" I noticed, he didn't flinch or grunt out of discomfort like he did when I disvirgined him.

I wound the leash around my left palm until it tugged his neck and grabbed his waist with my right hand. And just like that, I began to thrust deep into him.

Pam!! Pam!! Pam!!

Pam!! Pam!! Pam!!

Each time my groin hits his sore ass cheeks, he would wince, but the leash kept him in position.

Pam!! Pam!! Pam!!

He started groaning as I pegged him harder and harder. At some point, he wanted to fall forward, but the leash wouldn't let him.

Pam!! Pam!! Pam!!

Pam!! Pam!! Pam!!

His groans got louder, but this only stirred me to peg him even harder. I got so drawn into banging his ass to his loud cry so much so that neither of us noticed when Annabel came into the house. She walked right in and stood star-struck behind us, watching me peg her husband and watching him cry out loud.

"Oh my god!" Annabel gasped and let her bag fall to the floor. Only then did we know she had joined us in the room.

I looked back over my shoulder, just as Micheal did too.

Pam!! Pam!!

I thrust twice into his ass again.

"Hey, babe!" I said to Annabel.

"Martha!"

Pam!! Pam!! Pam!!

"I can't believe this!"

Pam!! Pam!! Pam!!

"I told you when you see him, you wouldn't believe what you are seeing, remember?"

Pam!! Pam!! Pam!!

Pam!! Pam!! Pam!!

"Micheal!" she came to the side and touched the bars of the cage to feel the material. She was overwhelmed by everything she saw—Micheal being pegged at the entrance of the cage with half of his upper body in, since I wouldn't get in there with him, his dress, his sore bottom and so on.

I momentarily ignored Annabel and gave her a show.

Pam!! Pam!! Pam!!

Pam!! Pam!! Pam!!

I got overboard and thrust deeply and forcefully into Micheal. I got very tough on him, tougher than necessary.

He began to cry out loud.

"Will you roll your waist for me, slave?"

"Yes, Goddess," he managed to speak, in broken speech. He rolled his waist as I kept banging his ass.

"Your husband is a slut now." I said to Annabel. She had her hands clasped on her mouth.

"I swear, I can't believe this. What the fuck!"

"Yeah, what fuck." I replied.

Annabel burst into laughter. Her laughter amused me and

slowed me down a bit as I joined her laughing, then I picked up pace again, holding the leash tight to prevent Micheal from falling forward due to the force of my thrusts.

Pam!! Pam!! Pam!!

Pam!! Pam!! Pam!!

Pam!! Pam!! Pam!!

I mentally got back into the scene and got super horny from fucking him. The base of the strap-on rubbed against my clit because I was fucking him so hard, and approaching climax.

Micheal was grunting. I was moaning. Annabel was watching.

Pam!! Pam!! Pam!!

I thrust harder and harder until I climaxed. My toes curled and I fell forward on his back as I cummed.

"Oh my god!" Annabel screams as she watched me sprawl on the floor.

Annabel's eyes were fixated on Micheal's asshole. The way it pulsed in and out amused her.

"You want to touch it? I suggested to her.

She nodded and sprang forward. The pulsing action sucked her finger in.

"What happened?" she asked, noticing all the welts and red swellings on his ass.

"I caned him."

She stared at every part of him and paused in shock.

"Oh, this is the cage. It's so small!"

"Yeah. I picked it at a moment I was angry at him. I was being vindictive."

What's this? She asked, touching the shock ring on his scrotum. The best way to tell her what it is, is to show her. Thankfully, the remote was with me.

Bzzzzzzzzz!!

"What the fuck, Martha!" she screamed and retracted her hand from the device. I laughed out loud.

"It's an electric shock ring, for electrifying his balls." I stretched my hand towards her, "Take, try it. Push the button."

Bzzzzzzzzzzzzzzzzzzzzzzzzzzzzzzzz!!

I thought I am the crazy one. Annabel collected the remote and pushed the button nonstop until Micheal's body wriggled on the floor of the cage. I screamed, got up and snatched the remote out of her hands. "Gosh, you want to kill him?"

She holds her hands out giggling and looking like she has no idea what just happened. "Is he gonna die?" she asks me, genuinely.

"Of course, he won't," I replied, laughing at her. And then she held out her hand at me, asking for the remote.

"Push and hold for just a few seconds, Anna, just a few seconds!" I reiterated and returned the remote.

Bzzzzzzzzz!! Bzzzzzzzzz!!

"Like this?"

Bzzzzzzzzz!!

"Yeah, like that."

Bzzzzzzzzz!!

"Haha, this is fun!"

Of course, it is. She goes on playing and pushing the button. Micheal jerked each time she sent shock waves to his balls.

Standing before Annabel and facing away, he bent forward and spread his ass cheeks, presenting his ass to her. He remembered to do that, as I instructed.

"What's he doing?"

"Showing you his ass."

◆ ◆ ◆

Annabel fell backwards, slamming her ass on the couch. She held the leash and Micheal went on his knees before her.

"He can worship your feet. I'll go serve lunch."

Micheal leaned forward at once and lifted her feet off the floor.

"Just relax and allow him to pamper you," I said to her.

She spread her toes out and rested her back, smiling at Micheal. As he started blow-jobbing her big toes, I turned around and went into the kitchen. I trust him to do an awesome job.

Annabel learns very fast. She has always been the brilliant one while I am the crazy one. By the time I return, the whole of her left foot was inside Micheal's mouth, almost tearing it apart.

"Anna!" I gasped.

"Don't 'Anna' me!" She replied, mimicking that line of mine and laughing.

"You are now a naughty girl."

"Yeah, I want everything." she proudly replied.

Spaghetti Bolognese for lunch. I'm sitting at the table and beckoning at Annabel to join me.

"How about sitting on his face and farting in his mouth while you enjoy this delicious meal?"

"You're the best sister in the world!" she happily replies.

Micheal knows the position too well. He sat on the floor beneath the table and reclined his head backwards on the chair.

"Will his neck break?" she asks me.

"It didn't break when I did that to him," I replied. "Just go down carefully on him, your weight will settle on him safely."

She held out her ass cheeks and slowly mounted his face.

"What's he doing?"

"Searching for your anus."

She sighed and bit her lips, "Wow."

She and I then began to dig into the lunch while Micheal rimmed her. "This feels a bit weird, she says to me.

"You will get used to it, won't you?"

Krrrrrrr Kbummmmmmm!!

Annabel suddenly ripped a fart into Micheal's mouth.

"Anna, I thought you said this is weird?" I asked her, jokingly.

"It is, but I love it." she replied, bouncing her ass on his face.

"I can tell his lips are sealed around your anus now. His goal is to catch your fart and swallow all of it, you might want to sit still a little..."

"Okay, okay..."

I enjoyed staring at her and seeing how overcome with joy she was. It's her first time dominating someone, and this someone happens to be her husband who was spinning out of control.

She rested her weight on his face and continued with lunch, but occasionally still playfully rolling her waist, but not breaking the contact between her anus and his mouth.

I asked her to look down and check his dick. While the size of the cage made it extremely difficult for his penis to swell at all, the proof of sexual excitement was still visibly observable. Pre-cum dripped from the tip of his dick.

"Is he enjoying this?"

"Yes," I replied, emphatically. "What pushed him into vices was boredom. He wanted some action in his life. Some high energy activity. Dominating him will satisfy his need to drift in that high energy state."

Annabel hummed and paid attention to my short Ted Talk.

Bzzzzzzzzz!!

I didn't know she still had the remote until she pushed the shock button again.

"Looks like that will be your favourite toy?"

"I love it!"

"There are ones designed for the neck too, just Ike the collar around his neck, but electro-."

"I prefer this one," she said raising her shoulders. "I prefer to shock his balls. It's more fun."

"Anna, it's my turn to say 'Naughty girl!'"

She giggled. "Haven't you said that already?"

"I don't know, I'm not sure."

Fffff Frk Fkrrrruummmpp!!
Fkkkkk Fkpkkkkkkkkkk!!

Annabel detonated five nasty ass bombs in Micheal's mouth.

"Damn. Was that too much?" she jokingly asks me.

"Is he complaining?"

"No. I don't hear him complaining."

"Same here."

She ripped farts in his mouth until we were both done with lunch and even continued to fart in his mouth afterwards.

"Ain't you coming over here?" I asked her, wanting to show her a page in a women's magazine.

"Can he follow me without breaking the seal?" she asked me, wanting to come over to the couch, but not willing to let go of the feeling of his tongue in her bumhole — not even for a few seconds.

"I guess if you walk slowly..."

"Alright, slave," she says to Micheal, "Follow me."

"Since you are the queen of all the mean ways with which one can treat men, you should know some device that would make this easy," she says to me, halfway between the dining set and the couch.

"Yes, there's a device. It's called a smother harness."

"Haha. You know them all!"

I chuckled and patiently waited for her to get beside me. Anna walked with her legs spread apart so as to accommodate Micheal's body under her. They made it over to the couch without breaking the seal between her anus and Micheal's lips.

"I can see you're going to do just fine with him," I mused.

She smiled and winked at me, "I learnt from the best; You! Martha. And even still learning."

Without a doubt, I am happy to be her mentor.

We argued over some shopping offers in the magazine. When we turned to another page, we were gossiping about some celebrity divorce that was trending, and then;

Fruuummmmmpp!!

"Ewww!" I sighed light-heartedly.

She is getting used to this faster than I thought she would. She didn't even flinch after ripping nasty farts into his mouth, nor pay him any attention. We chatted and enjoyed each other's company completely oblivious of Micheal's ordeal beneath her butt.

My mind flashed back to Annabel's call a few days back when I was in the club. I vividly remembered how she looked before me at the door to my house, in awe of just having escaped a violent episode in her own home.

She's back in that home now — as the boss of the maniac who is now as submissive as a lamb.

Her energy is renewed and she's taking her place as the queen of her home. It took just one person to bring this turnaround.

Yes. Me. My name is Martha. I bring glad tidings to women.

My phone buzzed. Wilfred calling.

"Hello, Martha."

His hoarse voice and the way he occasionally stammers pleasured my ears. He and his wife are part of my close circle of friends in the d/s world.

"And how's the man that got into trouble with you?" he says, not forgetting to ask after Micheal.

"He is fine, sitting under my sister's ass right now, and eating her farts."

His voice cracked, laughing.

"And the cage?"

"Oh, Wilfred, you were right. It's way too small for his dick."

"And you had to force it?"

"Like I said I would, yes, and it worked. He is wearing it right now."

"Oops. Poor soul."

Wilfred moves unto the reason he called.

"Freya is back. The rope class had to be brought forward to Wednesday night because Dr Alfred would be out of the country by Friday, which we initially planned. He has some urgent business abroad."

Annabel is staring at me now, listening to the conversation.

"You know, Martha, I wouldn't want you to miss this class. Dr Alfred asked after you."

The Almighty Alfred has a spot for me? Amazing! Now I can't miss that class.

"You could bring that chastity cage victim of yours," Wilfred says with his crooked voice, "Let's tie him up!"

"Haha!" I chortled. Martha stares at me curiously, having a hint that whatever was amusing me on phone has to do with domination, and probably Micheal.

"Wilfred, I am coming. And I am bringing him. Let's tie him up!"

Wilfred was elated.

"What is it, Martha?" Annabel impatiently asked me.

"We are going to a rope party. You and I.

And Michael!"

CHAPTER 8 – SHIBARI

"Rope party?" Annabel asked, looking lost like she just got invited to a NASA space program emergency meeting. She had no idea what in the world that means.

"It's a contemporary form of rope bondage that originated in Japan. For us, it's a form of art."

"Us?" She chuckled.

"Oh! Us — Kinky people."

"I guess I'm one now?"

"Yes. And Micheal too."

Some pictures on my phone came handy in explaining to her what rope play is all about, and then Anna cracked me up. She wanted to tie Micheal just based off pictures I showed her!

"Anna," I sighed, laughing hard, "When done well, rigging can be astonishingly beautiful. But when done badly, it can be dangerous."

"Rigging?" That's the art of tying. "It's a skill that should be learned properly, that's why you are coming to the rope workshop with me."

From that moment, Anna didn't stop talking about ropes until now that we just got out of the car and are standing in front of the dungeon.

"Is this it?" she asked, looking a bit confused.

"Yes, this is the dungeon."

"But it doesn't look like one!"

Guess what — Annabel is expecting to see a holding cell under a medieval castle!

No wonder she has been repeatedly mentioning the word.

Wilfred walked towards us to give a warm welcome to the 'Friends' I brought. I disappeared into the embrace of his wide shoulders. He noticed Annabel and Micheal laughed along with me. "What's funny?"

"My sister here thought I was bringing her to a middle-age dungeon! You know, with lanterns and branding irons and starvation cells!"

Wilfred smiles courteously at Annabel and blinks at me.

"Yeah, please meet my sister, Annabel."

He stretched his hand and shook hers gently.

"And this is Micheal, her husband."

He remains composed and stretches his hand at him also. "We are a diversity-friendly club," he says to him and Anabel. "We accept all gender types and sexual orientations."

"Ha, Wilfred," I burst into laughter, "He is a 'He!'"

Wilfred looked confused. He thought I came with two ladies. Annabel joined me in laughing.

"I turned him into a sissy maid, but he is a straight male." I turned my face at Micheal, "Show him your genitals, slave."

Micheal got very nervous, shy and vulnerable, but he bent down and rolled the gown up from the helm. It was a long one that reached his ankles.

When he rolled it up his waist and revealed his dick locked in that micro cage I bought from Wilfred, he got convinced.

He looked back at me in awe and winked involuntarily. "You enslaved your brother-in-law?"

I shrugged and slanted my head, "Yup!"

As we headed in, Freya came out and met us on the way. I introduced her to Annabel and Micheal and for whatever reason, she assumed 'Micheal' is now a unisex name!

When I dressed him up with the makeup and wig and told Annabel people would think he is female, she doubted me. Now she's just laughing and seeing for herself, how convincing, or rather, how believable feminization can be.

"Wilfred told me you are bringing a slave. Where is he?"

Annabel grins widely and says beneath her breath, "Here we go again."

I laughed at her as if to say I told you so. Yeah, here we go again.

"He is here," I said to Freya.

"Where?"

"Here," I repeated and snapped my fingers. Wilfred was smiling already.

Micheal rolled the gown upwards again and showed Freya his caged dick.

"What a cutie!" Freya commented, "He looks adorable."

I did nothing to prepare him for this embarrassment. His face flushed with shame. Freya noticed and tried to help him get his confidence back.

"He is new to this," I said to her, "But he is doing great already."

"Come," Freya said to me, "You might want to say hi to Dr Freya before the workshop starts."

My curiosity and interest in rigging gave me out at the last workshop, where my insightful questions stirred up the class and made Dr Freya notice me.

I'm turning up to him with my crew. He was pleased to see me. I introduced Annabel to her as my sister, and Micheal as our slave. He was also impressed with how I transformed him.

"You are brilliant and adventurous, I like that about you," a smile grew on his face and his eyes shined on me.

Yup! I jumped in my heart. Is this me here scoring another point with the phenomenal Dr Alfred?

My heart pounded and for some reason, I blushed shyly to his admiration.

"Thank you, Dr Alfred." I'm having a second and closer look at him and naughtily finding him quite cute. Should I be jealous of this blonde model that follows him around?

Allysa. 5"3. Slender.

She rested in the background with her heart-shaped face staring blankly. Even the girl is phenomenal too. This blank face will soon start emitting a wide spectrum of indescribable emotions when Dr Alfred's knots and ties come on her.

I enjoyed the time I spent with Dr Alfred, getting a peek into his life outside rope classes as he got a peek into mine too.

"We could make today's demonstration interactive, with you taking the stage with me, mirroring my moves on your sub. Is that a go?"

My heart skipped a beat. Dr Alfred and me on the stage? Yes, yes, yes!

Foot traffic and voices increased outside the room we were in with Dr Alfred. Guests are arriving and the live session would begin in just a matter of minutes. Dr Alfred swiftly gave me an overview of what he would be doing and guidelines on how to replicate his moves. Then we moved to the play area.

The stage was prepped already, with hanging bars and hooks and the likes. As part of the preparation, I made Micheal drink water to be hydrated to reduce the risk of injury.

Annabel closed in on me and tapped my waist.

"Isn't that Bishop Kuh?" she stealthily pointed at him.

"Yeah. He wants to learn how to tie demons," I playfully replied my excited sister.

She walked off touring the space and in a few minutes, came back to me after seeing some up-coming female rap artist.

"Is this thing so popular?" she asked.

"This lifestyle is for fine people. And besides, rope bondage is an art. Anyone who loves art can easily like it."

Now she's glad I brought her to the dungeon. She was having fun by herself, walking around, admiring dungeon equipment and even meeting people. The dungeon regulars could tell she was my sister and welcomed her.

She is now in my fetish world and she is liking it. In jest, she accused me of keeping this fun world away from her all this while.

"How should I have known you would love this, Anna?"

She frowned and exuberantly scurried away again. Seeing her flourish in this atmosphere brought joy to my heart. We would even be closer, now that she can resonate with me on this level.

The music theme for the event is heavy metal. Extended guitar solos and distortion quickly hyped up the energy in the room, exciting Annabel more than anyone else.

Dark lighting combined with the booming music, and Allysa steps on the stage. She alone just yet. She bowed to the audience and sat still. The ropes hadn't come on her then, but the session kicked off with it.

Her pose was sensational and attention-grabbing. Coupled with the music, we all got ready to see something heavenly.

All eyes on me as I stepped on the stage with Dr Alfred. Micheal came behind me.

Dr Alfred gave a ten minutes lecture before the rigging started. Alyssa took her dress off, leaving her bra and panties on. I signalled to Micheal and he took his clothes off.

As one would expect, a kinky audience responds to fetish things differently from how vanilla folks do. Micheal expected mock stares and remarks like he got he I took him to the clothing store, but here, it's the opposite. Undressing and revealing he was feminized was met with admiration from the audience. For once, he was proud of public play.

This made Annabel see everyone under that roof like a family and now understands why I used the word 'Us' in a previous conversation.

The rigging started and everyone paid rapt attention.

Each step we took got my soul more involved in this, as I stare at Micheal in that sweet suffering. I looped the rope around his left thigh and threw it over his shoulder. When I turned around and pulled on it, he groaned. It moved my soul.

I'm used to inflicting pain on men, but as he got in my ties, I could feel and identify with his vulnerability. Every pull, every loop, every tie reflected on his face. I felt so connected with his suffering.

Dr Alfred halts for a few seconds and faces the crowd;

"We are fetishizing pain, but the pain is not an end in itself. Yes, the pain may have to be very strong, but in context, the suffering the bunny is going through is a journey for both who is being tied and who is doing the tying."

Yes! That is right! I could only hope the audience understands Dr Alfred the way I do. His words are alive in my ears. Every breath Micheal took bothered me because I could hear him breathe. And now I see why there's so much attention given to learning Shibari, in comparison with learning other fetishes. One wrong pull and I could crush some nerves or break some bone. Everything has to be calculated. I have to know what I'm doing.

And that bit about journey? So true.

For a high-energy person like me, this event forced me to enter into this state where I had to be still. It's a sexual or erotic practice that is so complicated in knots over here and ties over there and yet as you proceed in it, is rich in simplicity.

I could feel the brokenness and deconstruction of his body. I held his neck and stared into his eyes just as Dr Alfred did to Allysa, and what did I see? — ultimate surrender! That always gets me horny!

I pulled the suspension rope downwards and Michael's body lifts off the floor. My heart beat rapidly in sync with his. I previously thought rigging was a chore for the rigger. Now I understand it's not a chore, but a journey the rigger embarks on with the rope bunny.

Micheal groaned as I pulled the rope lower. I tied it around the intricate design behind his back and stared at Annabel amidst the audience. I bet she can also feel what I'm feeling.

"The visual imagery is awesome," Dr Alfred says to the audience, "But you should also revel in the emotions it evokes."

I replicated Dr Alfred's every move and by the time we were done, Michael was hanging in the air. His hands are tied behind his back, legs folded and wide apart and rope through his butt crack and groins.

He was exactly in the same position Allysa was, only that in addition to the artistic agony he was in, he also panicked. His head was at the same level as my boobs while on my feet, so it was reachable. I patted him and spoke words to calm him down, as Dr Alfred taught me to do. Then we allowed the audience to draw in inspiration from the soulish display.

Although rope bunnies are mostly female, it is not unusual to see male bunnies. What is unusual is to see them in other forms of restraint or bondage other than rope. Micheal's dick was in a pitiable predicament — a rope bunny locked in an undersized chastity cage. This was something folks hadn't seen before. I was proud of Micheal. Annabel was proud of him. Wilfred and Freya were proud of me. Dr Alfred was proud of Micheal and me.

The audience spent the hour admiring the display. We carefully dropped the suspension afterwards and as Dr Alfred bonded with Allysa in a warm embrace, so did I with Micheal. Questions and answers were entertained, so were feedbacks. The heavy metal came back on afterwards and the room got noisy again.

I didn't foresee people coming up to me to chat with me about the session like they did with Dr Alfred. I basked in the glory and felt like a pro.

"That was amazing!" Annabel said to me, and then she threw her arms around Micheal too, and then she left him and wandered off with some of my friends who were excited to meet 'Martha's sister."

The way it looked to me, Annabel would probably do just fine here without my presence. Her energy and openness to things that she could very well still describe as' Strange' is simply just amazing. I knew she was in safe hands and would be fine, so I didn't bother about her. A lot was happening around me and in my mind to keep me occupied. I'm already feeling like a shibari guru, even though I had to copy every move I made.

The validation from Dr Alfred made my day. He, Allysa, Micheal and I retreated into the separate room he was received in and we conversed deeper. I got to interact more closely with Allysa too and she was as stunned by Michael's performance just as Dr Alfred was with mine. Wilfred and Freya joined us and the six of us spent some time together, munching strawberries and cream, and red wine.

Where is Annabel? Wilfred asked me. *Oh yes. Where the fuck is Annabel?*

"She's having fun somewhere, I bet."

"She seems to be settling in just fine."

"Yes, Wilfred. I didn't know she would blend in so well."

"I saw her with Rex, Robin and Elsie," Freya said.

"Ha!" I puffed, "My sister is having a session already?" They laughed at me as I went out to see what she was up to.

"Anna!"

Robin was strapped to the spanking bench and she was flogging him with Cat O'Nine Tails in her hand. She winked at me and continued flogging him

Robin is Elsie's submissive. Robin and Rex are friends. All three of them are my boon companions. I stood beside Elsie and watched Anna warm-up Robin's butt. That she was spanking someone other than Micheal gave her some thrill, and it also showed her that she was welcome to the family.

"She's quite impressive with it," Elsie quipped.

"Yeah, I've shown her a few things, practically."

"Oh, that's great."

Micheal slipped out of the room and joined me at the play area. He was elated to see Annabel spanking someone, and also, he saw that he was not alone.

He is new to submission, but he can draw comfort from knowing that what I broke him into is not an unpleasant situation, rather, it's a lifestyle some people enjoy. This helped him to loosen up even more, and if he had any hidden regrets about what he has now become, those regrets disappeared. He smiled watching Annabel. He was earlier on the stage as a performer, now it's his turn to watch and be entertained.

And even now, he is still enjoying some attention and validation.

From the spanking bench, they moved to the bondage bench, and then from that to St Andrew's Cross. Annabel wants to use everything, and she has a Mistress, her sub and her sub's friend willing to make that happen for her.

It is needless to say Annabel registered that evening, without having to go through the usual veto process. She was admitted on merit.

And Micheal? He too.

As far as I can tell, it was a great evening for everyone, but especially for Annabel, Micheal and me. Each of us had new experiences that evening. I got to perform on stage with a Shibari

Lord, Micheal finds out there are other real submissive men out here and sees it's a healthy lifestyle, not just some sad thing his wife's sister forced down his throat, and Annabel finds a family of kinky people.

We said goodbyes and got into the car. The drive home was loud for us three. We were talkative. The transition in Micheal's disposition was sharp. Unlike Annabel who looked forward to the event, Micheal didn't, since it was slated to be another embarrassing public humiliation for him. He felt that way up until getting on the stage and then things changed with the validation he got from the audience. And when I started tying him up, he became a model and got proud of submission.

He is happy now and proud of himself. He and Anna are asking me about the club events, how regularly they come up, what other kinds of events are hosted, how to book the dungeon for play, and many other questions which I was happy to answer.

Micheal's open acceptance intrigued Anna a lot and she was grateful to me for pushing them both into this.

While Micheal's hands were on the steering, I reached for his dick.

"Please, keep your eyes on the road," I said to him as I unlocked the chastity cage and tucked it in my wallet. Before we left the dungeon, I bought a bigger cage that's more appropriate for his dick size. I gave it to Anna and she smiled. I have broken him for her. She can now gradually start taking up responsibility in dominating him and nurturing him as her slave husband.

It was an eventful night for us. We showered and got on the bed, in nightgowns, all three of us. It was no longer a strange thing for

Micheal, rather, something to be adored, as he learnt from the reception he got at the dungeon.

Micheal, our pet. He lay in the middle of Anna and me, and we both caressed him as we slept off.

CHAPTER 9 – DOMINANCE AND SUBMISSION

It's a new day for Micheal, a new day in the sense of a new beginning. His countenance towards me is now that of gratitude, for the things I have put him through and what I have transformed him into. He confessed to me that he feels saved from his demons.

"I feel like a baby," he said, explaining to Anna and me on the bed. "I have a lot of things to learn and have to follow orders. It takes me back to my days as a child when I needed guidance for everything."

I nudged Annabel to listen to him carefully as he bared his soul. I had earlier told her she now has to actively dominate him daily, even when she isn't feeling like it — at least lightly.

"See it as 'nurturing' him. You just heard him confess he feels like a baby. He is your baby now," I clarified to Annabel.

Micheal nodded in agreement.

"What you are saying now is, even if he doesn't act unruly, I should still punish him?"

"Yes! That is exactly what I mean. Punishment in the BDSM world is not an unpleasant thing. It is an activity you will both enjoy. Let me ask you a question. Did Robin offended you before you spanked him in the dungeon?"

She giggled.

"Aha! You see what I mean now?"

"This will be fun for me, Martha."

I know it will be for her. Her excitement in the dungeon was enough proof of that. I just needed to correct that impression she had that her submissive husband has to do something wrong before she dominates him, going by the premise that it was his misbehaviour that prompted me to come to their house and break him into a submissive man.

"You already know one of the things you have to do to him regularly..."

"Spanking?" she jumped in.

"Yes, spanking. This type is called 'Maintenance spanking.'"

"Maintenance?" Anna giggled, "I like the sound of that."

"Bring your face, let's try that," she said to Micheal. He leaned closer to her and closed his eyes.

She slapped his face. And then she did again. And then a rain of soft slaps until I held her hands.

"Please, keep the venom," I jokingly said to her.

Micheal found his voice and said softly, "Thank you, Mistress."

It moved Anna and she hugged him at once. Now their relationship will be more loving than it was before. That the giving of pain and the receiving of it can lead to such transformation is phenomenal.

I fetched a saucer from the kitchen and got back on the bed.

"Let's see how much juice he has saved up. This is a reward for his good behaviour."

The embrace between them got his dick semi-erect, but when I held it, it grew to its full length in my hands. He leaned on Anna and she hugged him, pressing his face into her breasts while I pulled on his dick backwards from between his thighs and stroked him. He was being pleasured by two sisters.

The pleasure was a lot for his throbbing dick and I didn't want him to cum so soon, so I pinched the tip of his dick. That slowed things down a bit for him, but I resumed massaging his dick almost immediately.

"I'd like to watch him make out with your leg," I said to Annabel and asked Micheal to get on the floor. Annabel sat on the bed beside me and stretched her legs forward.

She clasped her ankles on his dick and he began to hump her

legs. It was a visually stimulating exercise for her and me. My main concern was his cum. I want him to cum in the saucer, hence monitoring his sexual excitement. I wore the dog collar on his neck and gave the leash to Annabel. That was the first article to come back on his naked body — the collar.

I positioned the saucer right behind Annabel's heels so that he would cum into it as I instructed. He humped her legs like he was having actual sex and cummed in the saucer as he rested on Annabel's legs and remained still while he poured his load out.

"That's a lot of cum!" Annabel cited.

"Chastity helps them achieve that. When you want him to blow a huge load like this, deny him orgasm for a few days."

"For how long can I keep his dick locked away in the cage, Martha?"

"Days, weeks, months. For as long as you want. But make sure you regularly remove for cleaning when you have him caged for long periods."

"What do we do with the cum?" Annabel asked.

"It's his. He will drink it."

He leaned forward on his knees and lapped it all. He drank a cup of water to energize him for the next task — worshipping Annabel's pussy.

He drove his face up her thighs. I pushed his face into her crotch and ordered him to sniff it the way he sniffs my ass, then I challenged him to show us how good he is with his tongue.

Within minutes, he got Annabel moaning in all different kinds of languages. She grabbed the shits and clasped her legs behind his shoulders.

He slurped on her pussy until she cummed. It was the best orgasm Anna ever had with him, according to her.

I snapped my fingers at him, "Get on her bumhole."

It's a paradise morning for Annabel. She lazily turned on her side and faced me, making her ass accessible to Micheal who got behind her and parted her ass cheeks apart to find her rosebud. He found it and stuck his mouth on it.

"Do you want to sleep?" I asked Anna, seeing she was looking sleepy, likely orgasm-inspired. I talked less and watch her eyes close. She slept off just as soon as Micheal began to lick her ass.

◆ ◆ ◆

The lazy morning began with orgasms, but a more energetic scene was about to begin — Annabel's first pegging session.

Walking into the house the other day to find me pegging Micheal was her first time of seeing that live, and she's excited about doing it too. She found it exciting that a woman can fuck a man in exactly the same manner men fuck women.

I wore the strap-on dildo on her and told her the importance of lube in pegging so she wouldn't ignorantly ruin his butt when I'm not with them.

I made him lube the strap-on and his asshole herself. She got it right. Next thing was for her to penetrate him and Annabel is asking for heavy metal music!

I laughed out loud. "You can't get the dungeon out of your head, can you?"

"No, I can't. Please give me heavy metal," Annabel insisted.

The naughty girl literally waited for me to find some heavy metal playlist online and blast through the home stereo before she would continue with the session.

What else does she want from the dungeon? Crowd? She has me for crowd.

Micheal knelt doggie-style at the edge of the bed. Annabel stood behind him and I guided the tip of the dildo unto his asshole.

"It's not going in!" Annabel complained. Was she expecting his asshole to suck the dildo in like a magnet?

"Push, Madam. Push it in. I just disvirgined him some days ago. His man cunt is still kinda tight."

I held her waist from behind and pushed forward slowly. Micheal grunted as each inch of the dildo made its way deep into his ass. I held her waist still and guided her in pulling out. I pushed her waist back in, and then pulled her out.

The next entry was just her. She penetrated him by herself and pulled out. She loved the exercise and repeated the move. This helped Micheal to mentally adjust to having his ass drilled.

I encouraged her to increase the pace and she did. She grabbed him by the waist and began to fuck his ass. At first, her thrusts and body movements were awkward, but it balanced in time and she began to swing well.

I heard my phone ring and checked to see it was Clara calling. It's been a few days since we last talked. I would have called her if not for getting so busy with putting Micheal in his place and giving his life a new direction. She just wanted to check on me.

"How is your sister now?" she asked. "Martha, are you fucking with someone?"

I chuckled. "My sister is fine. It's an issue she had with her husband, but that has been resolved. The sound you are hearing is my sister fucking her husband in the ass."

"Knowing how crazy you are, I shouldn't be shocked!" she responded, laughing wildly. "You change things everywhere you go!"

"Yes. I agree. I empower women."

She would hear the story when I get back to her.

Annabel felt more 'In-charge' and pegged Micheal hard to her satisfaction. She told me she would do this often to humble him. She saw that feeling of being conquered on his face after she was done pegging him.

He was to resume at his workplace by noon, so we allowed him to shower and get ready to leave.

At the dungeon, Anna also wandered to the toy store and now wants to go back to get more.

"That spanking bench, I want one."

I imagined how much spanking Micheal will get from now onwards. It's an activity Anna seems to like a lot.

We all left the house at the same time, Micheal to work, Annabel and me to the Dungeon.

◆ ◆ ◆

Wilfred was surprised to see us back so soon. When he learnt we came to shop for toys for Annabel, he found her more fascinating. The first thing we bought was the spanking bench. It was expensive, but Anna didn't mind paying for it. This with the cage I had already installed, "Your house will be a dungeon," I said to Anna.

"That's the dream," she replied.

Bullwhip. Cat O'Nine. Paddles. Shock ring. Nipple. Clamps and some other small toys. The next big equipment we bought was a queening chair for oral service. By the time we were done, it looked like we wanted to open our own store!

It was a big surprise for Micheal when he returned home to see all these 'Weapons' Annabel bought to use on him. And instead of getting scared, he was rather excited and joined us in arranging the toys.

Annabel took the chair at the table beside the bed away and replaced it with the queening chair. In that position, she would be using it a lot.

This evening would be fun again. Without instructing him to, Micheal went into the kitchen and reappeared with a plate of biscuits and two cups of juice for Annabel and me. None for himself. He only wanted to serve.

He was as interested in getting under the queening chair as much as Annabel was in getting on top of it. I opted to assume I'm not in the room with them, so I'd see how they would play in my absence.

Micheal sat on the floor and reclined his head backwards unto the queening chair. His head sank into the middle and his upturned face remained in the centre, at about the same level with the rest of the surface of the chair.

Annabel cracked her knuckles, took one wicked stare at him and positioned her ass over the chair. Slowly, she lowered her beautiful ass on his face, and asked herself, "Pussy or bumhole?"

She dropped her ass on his face and decided for bumhole. The smell of her ass wrapped around his nose and he sniffed to breathe because air supply was cut away by her bum. She adjusted her ass and there was no longer any trace of Micheal's head visible. After a minute, he threw his hands.

"Anna, let him breathe."

She stayed fifteen seconds more on his face before she stood up. Micheal gasped for air. Barely thirty seconds after, she sat on his face again and cut off his air supply. They both enjoyed the asphyxiation.

"And when I want to sit on his face for hours?"

"Then you have to sit right," I told her.

I got off the bed and helped her sit right on his face so that his nose was fitted in her ass crack, but could still manage to draw some air. I got back on the bed and chatted with her.

Frrrrrrrrrrrrrr!!

She broke wind on his nose and covered his entire face with her ass again.

"Anna?"

"I want him to take it all," she said in defence of her action. I sat back and watched and enjoyed doing so.

"Are you ok?" Annabel asked Micheal. He mumbled. I couldn't hear whatever he was trying to say, but then he raised his hands and pointed his index and middle fingers up.

"You see!" Anna says to me.

"I see you both are having fun. Enjoy!"

It didn't take long before he threw his hands in the air again and Annabel sat properly like I taught her too and allowed him to breathe.

She shifted backwards on the chair and placed her pussy over his mouth. "Lick me, slave."

Slave? Nice. She must have called him that before, but it

sounded anew in my ears, in light of her recent aggressiveness and taking charge.

Micheal threw his tongue up and began to lick her pussy. She got wet and her pussy juice leaked on his face. She asked me to help her get the flogger.

With it, she spanked his belly while he ate her pussy.

"The mornings and the evenings are for this, right?"

"Noted!" Annabel replies excitedly at the suggestion I hinted. She was smart enough to recognize that that wasn't a question.

"Orgasms every morning and every evening..."

"If you have a face to worship you, Anna, I don't see why that shouldn't be."

"Exactly!"

She whipped Micheal's thighs and charged him to work harder. It looked like for every stress he had taken her through in the recent past, she wanted to make her pay for it in a few hours.

I briefly lost track of the event with them both when I picked my phone to answer some chat messages. I was doing that and in a trice, I began to hear Anna moaning.

"Dominance is going to make you a very happy woman," I said to her.

Anna didn't hear me. Damn. Micheal must be doing a good job.

"Anna, Anna," I called her quietly, "You are drowning your slave in your pussy juice!"

She heard me and tried to open her eyes, but was too given into the pleasure. Her vagina soaked Micheal's face and I heard him groaning and struggling. She had an orgasm on his face before she could hold any other conversation.

"I want him to sleep in the cage," she said to me and stood off his face.

"It's your choice, Anna. If you want it so. So be it." The power is in her hands now and I will make her realize that.

She collared his neck and walked him into the cage. "This is where you sleep tonight, slave husband."

I giggled in the background, proud of what my darling Martha has become.

We both went into the kitchen and made dinner. We had always loved cooking together. Micheal ate his dinner in the cage and slept in there. The pillow I tossed in earlier was still there and would be useful for his comfort through the night. It had been a hectic evening for him, so we just allowed him lay his head down and sleep.

From the bed, Anna and I could see him since the cage is just a few feet away. He slept off. We did soon afterwards.

◆ ◆ ◆

"Good morning, Goddess!" Micheal said to me as I squat at the door of the cage. I rubbed his head and scratched his chin.

"Do you promise me you will be a good slave to my sister? You know how much I cherish her now and will fight for her safety. Her enemy is my enemy."

"Yes, Goddess, I will be a good slave to her, I promise!"

"Remember all I have taught you and improve on them."

He bowed to me and said, "Yes, Goddess."

"I'm leaving this morning."

"Goddess, please don't go!"

It felt so nice that he had gotten so used to me and wanted my presence in that house, and that I can understand. Given how violently I overpowered him and turned him into a slave, it's not unfathomable to find him tied to me in some way. But unfortunately, I have to leave. I have a house and a life outside of him and Annabel's house.

I left the cage door open and went into the bathroom. When I came out after bathing, I saw Micheal's face on the queening chair, waiting for my ass.

"What a cute little boy you are, Michael," I said to him as I sat down and mounted my ass on his face.

I picked my toys that Annabel no longer needs because she bought hers and stuffed them in my bag. Then I took a sit on Micheal's face and rubbed cream on my body. My stay here has been a successful one and they will both miss me.

He poked his tongue up between my thighs on my pussy, which was directly over his mouth. I managed to finish packing my bag before his tongue drove me to ecstasy.

I began to moan and secret my juice on his face. Eventually, my moans woke Annabel up.

Micheal's tongue is magical. Annabel is talking to me but I can't pay her any mind. I can only focus on the pleasure Michael's tongue is giving me.

He licked my pussy to orgasm and I cummed on his face. He owed me that orgasm. They both owed me, he and Annabel.

I readjusted my ass on his face and stuffed his nose with my anus.

"Morning orgasms?"

"Yeah, morning orgasms," I replied Annabel and winked at her. She sees I've packed my bag and attempted to make me change my mind about leaving.

"Anna," I chuckled, "This is not 'So soon,' I've been here for days."

She didn't listen to me and insisted this was me leaving so soon. I began doing my makeup, resolute that I would leave.

Brrr Braubbbbbbbpp!!

I loosened my anus on Micheal's nose.

"Sweetheart, I'll come back next weekend, ok," I begged and convinced her to let me leave, having to promise her a weekend before she accepted.

Down under my ass, Micheal is inhaling my farts deep into his lungs, since I cut part of his air supply away with my ass after farting, he had to actively inhale my farts to stay well and alive.

I press my lips together after applying lipstick on it and I feel my anus opening up. Silent wind blew out of it up Micheal's nose and I press my ass down on his face again. Some more torture alongside others to miss me with.

Turning Micheal into a slave and dominating him in their house has been fun. Annabel having him to serve her day and night everyday inspires me to find a live-in slave too. I have been dominating men and having exciting play sessions in and out of the dungeon, but having one that would live in my house, even if just for a few days at a time, is not something I considered until now that I see how cool that can be.

I ripped another fart in Micheal's nose and made him sniff it all, then I wore my skirt and stood off his face.

Annabel held me in a warm embrace and wouldn't let go.

"I love you, Martha. You are the best sister anyone can have. You are the best sister in the world."

I hugged her tightly too. "I love you, Annabel. Stay on top of your man, and any other one that comes your way."

She giggled, "Now that you have shown me the way, I surely will."

CHAPTER 10 – HIS NAME IS JASPER

Annabel washed my bathroom, wiped cobwebs off the ceiling of the car garage, but somehow managed to leave the kitchen cupboards open — all of them!

This is how you know if Anna has been in a place. Cupboards, wardrobes, cabinets — it's a sin for her to close them. If she does, something cataclysmic might occur and the world might end.

I slammed myself on my bed and rolled on my back. Staring at the ceiling, I began to think about the event of the past week. Club G4. Annabel. Michael. The shibari session with Dr Alfred. It has been an eventful week. One that has impacted me profoundly.

In such a short time, Annabel has risen from a novice to a dominatrix. She still has a lot to learn, but with me and the dungeon club to guide her, she will do just fine.

Micheal is done with vices and substances, having had that replaced with something deeper and more meaningful. He now finds fulfilment in servitude. Rest for his soul, rest for Annabel's. Fun for his soul, fun for Annabel's.

And me? Someday soon, I may get to host a Shibari class too. The live practice with Dr Alfred boosted my confidence a lot and inspired my soul.

And Clara? I dialled her number on my phone. She is happy to know we can hang out again. Luckily, it's another weekend already and we are both free.

"I wished you came along, Clara. It was a wilder version of what I did to that dude at the club."

"Next time there will be some action, please remind me to tag along," Clara groused.

"Hmm, Clara..."

"I'm listening..."

The week in Annabel's house has led me to decide I want a Live-in slave. But who?

"Clara, we will be having our own show here, something more of a permanent arrangement."

"Huh?"

"Yeah, you heard me right, girl." I scratched my head and did a quick think. I can get a submissive from the club, but that would be boring for me. I want someone like Micheal, someone I will break with my own hands and mould into what I want.

The initial resistance, the naivety, the culture shock, how they begin to adjust and other newbie effects are all part of the fun for me. Even more than just being a part, they are the core of how I like my d/s experiences.

"G4 tonight?" I asked Clara.

"Yes, please. Let's rock and roll!"

"Deal."

◆ ◆ ◆

There is always an endless supply of submissive males. In chat rooms, pubs, everywhere. Thoughts start taking form in my mind. Finding my own live-in slave can't be that difficult, not for someone like me.

It's 5 pm and I should start getting ready to meet up with Clara. I showered and got my skin shinning and smelling nice with whipped body butter.

"Yes, I'm getting on the road now," I said to Clara.

"Alright. I just got on the road here."

"Okay, Clara."

We ended the call and I tucked my phone into my wallet. The denim jeans trousers I picked for this evening is very tight, but I forced it up my legs.

No bra this evening. It's 'No bra' Friday for me, so I got comfortable in a black T-shirt, proudly bearing imprints of my nipples. I grabbed my purse and dashed out of the house.

It's beautiful weather this evening. Purple and pink clouds in the vast expanse of the sky above complemented the colourful light bulbs beneath. Foot traffic is building and its also a bit windy this.

Where is Clara? I didn't want to call but find her myself. As I stare around, I enjoy the sight of other beautiful people. The usual hippy half-clad girls screaming in their soprano voices, a couple of old ladies who won't let old age retire them from feeling young again, some decent gentlemen on the hunt for girls, beautiful people everywhere, around G4 and other clubs on the street.

Something tickles my right ear. I tickle it and keep looking. The 'something' tickled my ear again and I turned around as I shove my finger in,

"Hey, you!" Clara says from behind and throws the red feather on the floor.

We hugged tightly and headed in.

"Hello, ladies!"

Clara and I turn sideways. It's Ellis.

"Where have you been?"

Ellis likes to see us often, like every other night, which practically is impossible, but we show up as often as we can.

"We are here now," Clara says to him happily. He pulls us closer to himself and makes us sit on the tall stools by the bar. He's going to buy us drinks, like he does all the time.

"Martha, you sent that guy away."

"Which guy?" I asked, feigning ignorance. Clara bends her face and stares at me from beneath her brow.

"You know who."

Of course, I know who. Clara knows who. Ellis knows who. We all know who. I just hate to think I bullied someone, but I love it.

"Whatever I did was in service to Womanity," I say to Ellis' face.

"Has he been here since then?" Clara asked him.

"Nope! Not by any chance," Ellis replied. Clara turned her face on me.

"See, you chased the poor guy away."

"But he is around," Ellis quipped.

"Where?" I asked curiously.

"Please don't tell her!" Clara jokingly blurts.

"Do you want her to bust my balls?

"Haha! I'm the house bully now eh?"

Ellis is our go-to guy here. He knows everything happening around the block and always has authentic information. I threw a tequila shot down my throat.

"Ellis, where?" I snarled at him.

He covered his genitals with both hands and said to me, "Calm down, I will tell you."

He and Clara laughed at me. Meanwhile, I've been catching glimpses at me from every angle. They remember the kick-ass girl. But back to Ellis;

"Come on, man, don't be ridiculous," I said, giggling.

Hmm. Ellis. Ellis. My mind wanders briefly. No. I will prefer the dude I stripped naked. Mr Crushed Balls. I already have a start with him. But if eventually, I will break Ellis too, well then, maybe for Clara. I stared at Clara and swallowed my thoughts.

"What, Martha?"

"Nothing."

"You sure? I saw a streak on your face, and I know you, Martha."

Ha. Am I so readable? No worries. That thought is still for me alone, for now.

"He has been to Rhodes twice since then."

"Rhodes down the street?"

"Yep."

"Poor dude," Clara chips in.

"You both left early. Did you get to find out how he left?

"No, but you are about to tell us."

"Man was so down, he didn't know how to get up."

Given the circumstances, naked, in pain, shamed in public, I could imagine how tough that must have been for him.

"Barman gave him a knicker, it was bigger than him and didn't fit, but that was enough to help him get on the way home."

Clara and I laughed.

"To be honest, his dick appeared small!"

He, Clara and I laughed hysterically. His dick might just be average-sized, but under the intense pressure I subjected it to, it's normal for it to shrink. I saw that happen with Micheal's dick too.

"We will check on our man," I told Clara. "I want to lay my eyes on him again, just to see how he is faring."

"Just to see?"

I could just want to see how he is faring, no doubt, but in this case, Clara is right. She knows I desire to do more than just see.

I moved on him the first time because he deserved it. My intervention was needed to stop him from harassing a lady. But now that he has, or must have learnt his lessons, how do I move on him unprovoked? I surely can't follow him around hoping to catch him in a transgression.

For this, I don't need a transgression. I don't need him to do any wrong. I just want to take him and make him mine. Is that impossible? Shouldn't be.

We got off the bar stools and sat on the padded chairs around a table. Smirnoff Ice for us both.

I couldn't toss thoughts about the stranger guy out of my mind, and the rest of the time we spent in G4 would have felt longer than it was, but for Clara;

"Your sister's husband..."

Yes. My Sister's husband. "His name is Michael," I began. There's no way we would have skipped this gist.

Clara shifted on her chair and dabbed her nose with a tissue. "No struggle at all?"

"None. His balls are big. They're the biggest I've seen. It makes it very painful for him."

Clara burst into laughter.

"I swear, they're almost the size of what they use in the English Premier League!"

"Premier League balls?" Clara retorted, laughing so hard.

"Oh my, you should have seen me on the pitch with the balls, I'm good!"

"Oh, yeah!"

Ellis sees us laughing and having fun and comes over to hang out with us. "I thought, that was just a one-time thing you did to that guy," he said to me.

"Something tells me you would love to be dominated."

"No way," Ellis humorously rejects the suggestion.

"The thought is always scary for you men at first, but when you get deep into it, you'd get addicted."

"Addicted? Not to this please."

"Tell that to Micheal who is now in love with worshipping his wife."

We began a debate on female domination. The topic is interesting for me, not just because it's femdom, but because it involves Ellis and Clara, which I think might play this game well.

The spark? They don't see it. But I do, and I'm guessing if something doesn't happen naturally between them, they might need a push. It might be me who will give that push. But I'm decided to just watch for now, until Clara wants a sub seriously. When I'm ready, I will go for his balls.

I raised my right foot and dropped it right on his groin as we continued blabbing about men and making them bow. Ellis acts like he didn't see or feel that.

I shook my head. This is the person who just swore 'No way?'

"So, how did Annabel feel about you taking Micheal's anal virginity?" Clara asked.

"For the love of God, you fucked your sister's husband?"

"Yup."

"How? You don't have a dick, Martha..." Ellis is confused. Clara keeps rolling her eyes and laughing at Ellis' naivety.

"It's called a strap-on. It's an artificial dick we wear to fuck men in the ass. You know, men like you."

Ellis laughed and jumped off the chair.

"Come on man, calm down!" I said to him. We were enjoying his company, but the statements are getting too hot for him to take. I could see that he somehow reveres me now, though he tries to conceal that.

"You are crazy, Martha."

"I know, but sit down, don't be scared," I replied, laughing out loud.

He managed to sit, and I dropped my foot on his groin as I did earlier, but didn't take a jab at him again just so I don't scare him away. Eventually, his friend showed up and he had to excuse himself.

I smiled and trailed him with my eyes as he walked away.

"I will break you, Ellie, when the time comes," I said softly.

"Are you kidding me?" Clara asked, laughing wildly.

"No, I'm not."

"Damn!"

"Yeah, damn."

Just then, my phone rang. My sister — Annabel.

Memories flooded my mind. The last time she called me like this, I was here in G4, having a good time, and then I heard the distress in her voice. I rose to the challenge and did what I know how to do best. Did it work?

Her voice is fine this evening, and full of life, but that's not all. She sounds unusually excited.

"Anna! What's going on?" I asked.

"It's Micheal!"

"What about him?"

"He is naked on his knees, at my feet. Bought me a new car!

"Yippee!" I screamed. Clara wonders what's responsible for my excitement.

"Volvo XC40. He says 'Just to appreciate me.'"

How else can he thank her for her dominance?

"I don't know how he pulled it off, but I didn't think this was something he could afford right now. But he just did."

"He wants you to know how much he appreciates your dominance over him. The way you spank him, the way you use him for your pleasure. You are meeting a deep need in his life, Anna, and he is grateful for it."

"God! How did you know that, Martha? Those were his exact words!"

Yup. I'm a genius. I know things, haha.

"Micheal bought Anna a car," I quickly told Clara to ease her curiosity while still on the phone with Annabel.

"Oh my!" Clara gasps and slants her head.

"Thank you, Martha. That's all I can say right now. I love you more than anything!"

Micheal's devotion to her is beyond what she can articulate at the moment. She's amazed at how submissive he has become. "I am all he thinks about," Anna says, talking loudly and happily."

"When are you coming over? Let's celebrate!"

Haha. Yes, we should do that. "Mind if I bring a friend?"

"Clara? Please bring her." She knows Clara is my number one buddy.

"Yes, Clara."

Clara is happy about the invite. Now she will get to see for herself, everything she has heard about Micheal and their now female-led marriage.

Clara and I ordered more drinks and made merry. In all that excitement, the thoughts of Mr Crushed Balls didn't slip by.

I tapped my fingernails on the table as I nodded my head incoherently to the club music.

"Rhodes?"

"Yeah."

We were done chilling at the club, but Rhodes first before we head home.

"What's amusing you two?" Ellis says at the exit, holding a can of beer.

"Something that froze your guts!" I replied sharply, not sparing him. He shrugged and smiled. Ellis is a good friend of ours, and we like him.

"Home?" he asks as if to verify his thoughts.

"Rhodes."

"I knew it, I hope you don't find him," he says, laughing.

I threw punches at his chest and pushed him out of the way.

"You had better hope we find him, else, you'd be taking his place."

"Ahh, Mon," he says in his Scottish accent.

We got in the car and I drove to Rhodes, just a few blocks down on the same street. We don't have a lot of time but just wanted to see if we would be in luck and find him.

Rhodes is smaller than Club G4, hence, finding him should be easier. We stayed in the car for a little while and looked out, running perimeter surveillance. We didn't see Mr Crushed Balls.

We were about stepping out of the car when Clara held my shoulder and pointed at someone on blue jean trousers and white Polo shirt, "Is that not him?"

I narrowed my vision and squinted my eyes. "That looks like him. Yes. That's him!"

We stepped out of the car and approached him. He stood facing our direction and recognised me easily.

At that moment, he surprised us both. He fled!

"Hey, come on man, I come in peace!"

I don't see why he should have been so scared that he ran into someone and fell. It's not cool. Makes me feel like a terrorist.

He would have disappeared easily if he wasn't so afraid. But as he got up, he ran into someone else again and fell to the ground. I hurried up to quickly catch up with him before he stands up. I hunkered down.

"Hey, dude, calm down. Calm the fuck down," I said to him as I unzipped his fly and reached for his balls, again.

"Relax, I come in peace." I clasped my hand around the base of his scrotum. He looked frightened and remained speechless.

Clara catches up with us and stays standing.

"Now let's stand up, shall we?"

Following my prod, he rose to his feet just as I stood straight too, without losing the grip on his balls. Only that this time, I didn't squeeze.

"My name is Martha, and this is my friend, Clara. What is your name?"

His chest heaved up and down. A few people were looking at us, but I had controlled the scene to make it less dramatic, only that anyone standing close could see I was holding him by the balls. His breaths were rapid and he looked confused about my seemingly friendly utterances despite dominantly holding his scrotum in my hand.

Because I don't like repeating myself with submissives, or people I intend to groom as submissives, I reminded him the question I asked with a little pressure on his balls and smiled at him, raising my eyebrows.

"My name is Jasper."

He is still fearful, but perhaps because I'm not causing him pain as I did on my first encounter with him, his dick begins to rise. I felt its heat as it hung over the back of my hand.

"Say 'Hi' to my friend, Clara."

"Hi!" he said to Clara and turned his fear-gripped face at me. Clara smiled and shook her head.

"Please, I haven't bothered any woman since then. I swear!"

I chuckled. poor soul. I taught him a lesson that day.

"I know, sweetheart. I know you have been a good boy. That's why I came looking for you."

His heartbeat is still rapid, but he felt relieved hearing that.

"Come with me."

I led him back to my car without letting go of his scrotum. We were now away from the crowd.

I jerked his scrotum towards me so that there was more tension on it, but still didn't put him in excruciating pain like I did that day. He shouldn't even feel any pain now, perhaps just minor discomfort, or at worst, very little pain. I wanted to be nice to him this time.

His eyes darted in all directions. He couldn't keep his gaze on me for long, out of fear.

"I know you are wondering what is it I want?"

He nodded. I knew. That expression was on his face, but he was scared to give voice to it.

"Jasper. I like submissive men. I want you to be my slave."

"Your slave?"

"Yes. My slave. I want you to be my slave, and I will be your Mistress."

"Hmmm," he puffed. I helped him to think about my proposition my making my grip on his balls more firm.

"You mean like BDSM slave?"

"Yes. BDSM. I want you to be my kinky slave."

His dick grew to its full length and shot out of the zip. Clara gasped and held her hand on her lip. "He is hard!" she says.

"That's all the answer I need right there, Clara."

"Come on, don't be shy. This is who you are," I said to him. He got shy and was looking away.

"Talk to me, Jasper."

"Yes, I will be your slave, Mistress."

"And I will be your Goddess."

"Yes, Goddess Martha. I want to be your slave."

I let go of his balls. "Bow and worship me!"

As if it was just us three out there, he paid no mind to whoever could be watching. He went on his knees and bowed at my feet. "I worship you, Goddess Martha."

"Wow! Just like that?" Clara gasped.

"Yes, just like that," I replied, smiling at her.

I carefully placed my foot on Jasper's head.

"Your worship is received, slave."

ABOUT THE AUTHOR

Author Dixit

Author Dixit writes Femdom Stories on humiliation and degradation.

BOOKS BY THIS AUTHOR

Learning From Our Neighbour

In the bid to be their brother's keeper, a vanilla couple find their way into their neighbour's apartment and what they saw not only shocked them, but also changed the course of their marriage.

One hell of a discovery — exciting for the wife, but threatening to the husband.

Max is bothered about Hailey's rapidly growing thirst for the odd demonstrations playing out before them.

The only way to perish the thoughts in Hailey's heart is for them both to leave immediately, but there is a problem;

Not only Hailey is hooked on the display, but even Max himself is also curious and wants to see more, risking dancing around a fire he wouldn't like to spread into their home!

The Counsellor

As it is mostly with women who get married to patriarchal figures, the weight of marriage started wearing Amaya out. While Donald grew stronger, she grew weaker and weaker until she couldn't take it anymore.

Then she met Dr Lisbon of Lisbon Counseling.

And then a simply beautiful woman took on a journey that transformed her into a Goddess over her husband.

Like Father, Like Son

Many months after turning her boyfriend into her slave, for some reasons, Tacha began to get bored of him, despite the fact that he was serving her well and giving her his best. She was growing wild and wanted some new adventure. Something super crazy.

Her decision on who she wanted as her new slave totally mortified Frodd; His father!

Aunty Margaret

After the death of her husband, Margaret Davids inherited her rich husband's properties and businesses. She became a wealthy woman and joined the league of high-value women in the city.

She has everything she wants in abundance, except for one thing; pleasure.

The Highway Women's Club catered to her pleasure amongst other things, but it just wasn't enough to meet her unique needs.

She wanted a slave that would please her in offering degrading services, but just couldn't bring herself to opening her arms and her home to a total stranger.

Someday, she got a distress call and saw the opportunity inherent in it.

This story is about how a kinky old woman breaks her favourite darling years ago into her slave.

Excerpt:

He made it to Aunty Margaret's house in no time. He couldn't believe the house the address led him to. It was a luxurious white mansion covering his view. He doubted if that was indeed her house, and if it was, how was she able to afford such an estate.

It was obvious he was expected. He was jolted out of his awe-struck surprise trance with the sudden appearance of Aunty Margaret, her alms wide open, beckoning for a hug, and a sweet voice saying to him,

"Welcome, little Daniel!"

He ran into her alms and hugged her tightly. She pressed him into her body and he was baptized into her smell.

"Only that you ain't so little again, you are now a grown man!"

"Well, yes, but I will always be your little Daniel!"

"Aww, you are still as cute as you used to be. I'm glad that didn't change. Come here baby boy, you are home now."

She clipped her left hands around his waist and walked him into the house.

"This is a Mansion! You live in a mansion, Aunty Margaret?"

He couldn't hide how amazed he was, but he was very happy seeing her in such an estate, it meant she very much has the power to turn his life around.

Made in the USA
Columbia, SC
04 January 2022

53423675R00107